who made
you a
princess?

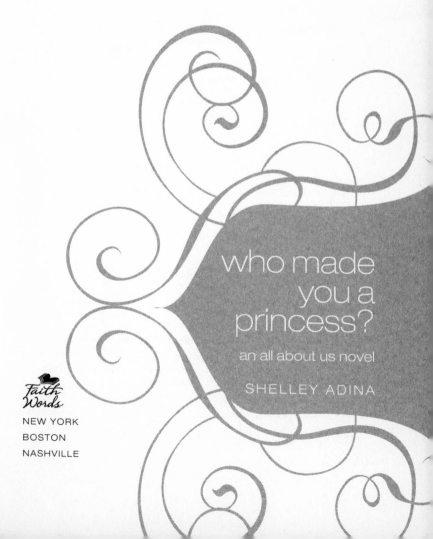

who made
you a
princess?

an all about us novel

SHELLEY ADINA

Faith
Words

NEW YORK
BOSTON
NASHVILLE

Scripture quotations marked KJV are taken from the King James Version of the Bible.

Scripture quotations marked NIV are taken from the HOLY BIBLE, NEW INTERNATIONAL VERSION®. Copyright © 1973, 1978, 1984 International Bible Society. Used by permission of Zondervan. All rights reserved.

The "NIV" and "New International Version" trademarks are registered in the United States Patent and Trademark Office by International Bible Society. Use of either trademark requires the permission of International Bible Society.

FaithWords
Hachette Book Group
237 Park Avenue
New York, NY 10017

Visit our Web site at www.faithwords.com.

The FaithWords name and logo are trademarks of Hachette Book Group.

Printed in the United States of America

First Edition: May 2009
10 9 8 7 6 5 4 3 2 1

Library of Congress Cataloging-in-Publication Data

Adina, Shelley.
  Who made you a princess? / Shelley Adina. — 1st ed.
    p. cm.
  Summary: The daughter of a wealthy businessman, Shani Hanna thought her parents sent her to school at Spencer Academy to groom her for a career in her father's company, but when she discovers that they instead want her to marry the son of a Middle Eastern sheikh, she must insist that she has other plans.
  ISBN 978-0-446-17962-1
  [1. High schools—Fiction. 2. Dating (Social customs)—Fiction. 3. Princes—Fiction. 4. Christian life—Fiction.] I. Title.
  PZ7.A261147Wh 2009
  [Fic]—dc22   2008031354

For Patty and Jennifer

acknowledgments

My thanks to my neighbor Patty and her daughter Sharron for letting me transplant bits of them straight into Shani, making her a character I love. Patty, it's your fault my girl craves sweet-potato pie.

Buckets of thanks go to Patricia Woodside for her grace and care over the beginning of this manuscript, and for encouraging me in ways even she doesn't know. Thanks likewise to Terri Haynes and Sherri Lewis, who gave me answers I didn't know the questions to, and who were very patient with my ignorance. I still think I could have gotten away with the hockey, though.

Thanks to Nicki Reidel, CEO of Black & White Design and owner of La Maison Angelique, who happily answered my questions about boutique vineyards and the grape harvest.

And to my BFF Heather Graham, who over the years of our friendship has educated me on oil-well abandonment, never suspecting I'd use it in a story someday.

And thanks as always to Jeff. You're the biggest reason why, as Lissa's T-shirt says, life is good.

who made
you a
princess?

And when he went out the second day, behold, two men of the Hebrews strove together: and he said to him that did the wrong, Wherefore smitest thou thy fellow? And he said, Who made thee a prince and a judge over us?
—*Exodus 2:13–14 (KJV)*

Choose my instruction instead of silver, knowledge rather than choice gold, for wisdom is more precious than rubies, and nothing you desire can compare with her.
—*Proverbs 8:10–11 (NIV)*

chapter 1

NOTHING SAYS "ALONE" like a wide, sandy beach on the western edge of the continent, with the sun going down in a smear of red and orange. Girlfriends, I am the go-to girl for alone. Or at least, that's what I used to think. Not anymore, though, because nothing says "alive" like a fire snapping and hissing at your feet, and half a dozen of your BFFs laughing and talking around you.

Like the T-shirt says, life is good.

My name's Shani Amira Marjorie Hanna, and up until I started going to Spencer Academy in my freshman year, all I wanted to do was get in, scoop as many A's as I could, and get out. College, yeah. Adulthood. Being the boss of *me*. Social life? Who cared? I'd treat it the way I'd done in middle school, making my own way and watching people brush by me, all disappearing into good-bye like they were flowing down a river.

Then when I was a junior, I met the girls, and things started to change whether I wanted them to or not. Or maybe it was just me. Doing the changing, I mean.

Now we were all seniors and I was beginning to see that all this "I am an island" stuff was just a bunch of smoke. 'Cuz I was not like the Channel Islands, sitting out there on the hazy horizon. I was so done with all that.

Lissa Mansfield sat on the other side of the fire from me while this adorable Jared Padalecki look-alike named Kaz Griffin sat next to her trying to act like the best friend she thought he was. Lissa needs a smack upside the head, you want my opinion. Either that or someone needs to make a serious play for Kaz to wake her up. But it's not going to be me. I've got cuter fish to fry. Heh. More about that later.

"I can't believe this is the last weekend of summer vacation," Carly Aragon moaned for about the fifth time since Kaz lit the fire and we all got comfortable in the sand around it. "It's gone so fast."

"That's because you've only been here a week." I handed her the bag of tortilla chips. "What about me? I've been here for a month and I still can't believe we have to go up to San Francisco on Tuesday."

"I'm so jealous." Carly bumped me with her shoulder. "A whole month at Casa Mansfield with your own private beach and everything." She dipped a handful of chips in a big plastic container of salsa she'd made that morning with fresh tomatoes and cilantro and little bits of—get this—cantaloupe. She made one the other day with carrots in it. I don't know how she comes up with this stuff, but it's all good. We had a cooler full of food to munch on. No burnt weenies for this crowd. Uh-uh. What we can't order delivered, Carly can make.

"And to think I could have gone back to Chicago and spent the whole summer throwing parties and trashing the McMansion." I sighed with regret. "Instead, I had to put up with a month in the Hamptons with the Changs, and then a month out here fighting Lissa for her bathroom."

"Hey, you could have used one of the other ones," Lissa protested, trying to keep Kaz from snagging the rest of her turkey-avocado-and-alfalfa-sprouts sandwich.

I grinned at her. Who wanted to walk down the hot sandstone patio to one of the other bathrooms when she, Carly, and I had this beautiful Spanish terrazzo-looking wing of the house to ourselves? Carly and I were in Lissa's sister's old room, which looked out on this garden with a fountain and big ferns and grasses and flowering trees. And beyond that was the ocean. It was the kind of place you didn't want to leave, even to go to the bathroom.

I contrasted it with the freezing wind off Lake Michigan in the winter and the long empty hallways of the seven-million-dollar house on Lake Road, where I always felt like a guest. You know—like you're welcome but the hosts don't really know what to do with you. I mean, my mom has told me point-blank, with a kind of embarrassed little laugh, that she can't imagine what happened. The Pill and her careful preventive measures couldn't all have failed on the same night.

Organic waste happens. Whatever. The point is, I arrived seventeen years ago and they had to adjust.

I think they love me. My dad always reads my report cards, and he used to take me to blues clubs to listen to the musicians doing sound checks before the doors opened. That was before my mom found out. Then I had to wait until I was twelve, and we went to the early shows, which were never as good as the late ones I snuck into whenever my parents went on one of their trips.

They travel a lot. Dad owns this massive petroleum exploration company, and when she's not chairing charity boards and organizing fund-raisers, Mom goes with him everywhere, from Alaska to New Zealand. I saw a lot of great shows with whichever member of the staff I could bribe to take me and swear

I was sixteen. Keb' Mo', B.B. King, Buddy Guy, Roomful of Blues—I saw them all.

A G-minor chord rippled out over the crackle of the fire, and I smiled a slow smile. My second favorite sound in the world (right after the sound of M&Ms pouring into a dish). On my left, Danyel had pulled out his guitar and tuned it while I was lost in la-la land, listening to the waves come in.

Lissa says there are some things you just know. And somehow, I just knew that I was going to be more to Danyel Johnstone than merely a friend of his friend Kaz's friend Lissa, if you hear what I'm saying. I was done with being alone, but that didn't mean I couldn't stand out from the crowd.

Don't get me wrong, I really like this crowd. Carly especially—she's like the sister I would have designed my own self. And Lissa, too, though sometimes I wonder if she can be real. I mean, how can you be blond and tall and rich and wear clothes the way she does, and still be so nice? There has to be a flaw in there somewhere, but if she's got any, she keeps them under wraps.

Gillian, who we'd see in a couple of days, has really grown on me. I couldn't stand her at first—she's one of those people you can't help but notice. I only hung around her because Carly liked her. But somewhere between her going out with this loser brain trust and then her hooking up with Jeremy Clay, who's a friend of mine, I got to know her. And staying with her family last Christmas, which could have been massively awkward, was actually fun. The last month in the Hamptons with them was a total blast. The only good thing about leaving was knowing I was going to see the rest of the crew here in Santa Barbara.

The one person I still wasn't sure about was Mac, aka Lady Lindsay MacPhail, who did an exchange term at school in the spring. Getting to know her is like besieging a castle—which is totally appropriate considering she *lives* in one. She and Carly are tight, and we all e-mailed and IM-ed like fiends all summer, but I'm still not sure. I mean, she has a lot to deal with right now, with her family and everything. And the likelihood of us seeing each other again is kind of low, so maybe I don't have to make up my mind about her. Maybe I'll just let her go the way I let the kids in middle school go.

Danyel began to get serious about bending his notes instead of fingerpicking, and I knew he was about to sing. Oh, man, could the night get any more perfect? Even though we'd probably burn the handmade marshmallows from Williams-Sonoma, tonight capped a summer that had been the best time I'd ever had.

The only thing that would make it perfect would be finding some way to be alone with that man. I hadn't been here more than a day when Danyel and Kaz had come loping down the beach. I'd taken one look at those eyes and those cheekbones and, okay, a very cut set of abs, and decided here was someone I wanted to know a whole lot better. And I did, now, after a couple of weeks. But soon we'd go off to S.F., and he and Kaz would go back to Pacific High. When we pulled out in Gabe Mansfield's SUV, I wanted there to be something more between us than an air kiss and a handshake, you know what I mean?

I wanted something to be *settled*. Neither of us had talked about it, but both of us knew it was there. Unspoken longing is all very well in poetry, but I'm the outspoken type. I like things out there where I can touch them.

In a manner of speaking.

Danyel sat between Kaz and me, cross-legged and bare-chested, looking as comfortable in his surf jams as if he lived in them. Come to think of it, he *did* live in them. His, Kaz's, and Lissa's boards were stuck in the sand behind us. They'd spent most of the afternoon out there on the waves. I tried to keep my eyes on the fire. Not that I didn't appreciate the view next to me, because trust me, it was fine, but I know a man wants to be appreciated for his talents and his mind.

Danyel's melody sounded familiar—something Gillian played while we waited for our prayer circles at school to start. Which reminded me . . . I nudged Carly. "You guys going to church tomorrow?"

She nodded and lifted her chin at Lissa to get her attention. "Girl wants to know if we're going to church."

"Wouldn't miss it," Lissa said. "Kaz and his family, too. Last chance of the summer to all go together."

And where Kaz went, Danyel went. Happy thought.

"You're not going to bail, are you?" Carly's brows rose a little.

It's not like I'm anti-religion or anything. I'm just in the beginning stages of learning about it. Without my friends to tell me stuff, I'd be bumbling around on my own, trying to figure it out. My parents don't go to church, so I didn't catch the habit from them. But when she was alive and I was a little girl, my grandma used to take me to the one in her neighborhood across town. I thought it was an adventure, riding the bus instead of being driven in the BMW. And the gospel choir was like nothing I'd ever seen, all waving their arms in the air and singing to raise the roof. I always thought they were trying to deafen God, if they could just get up enough volume.

So I like the music part. Always have. And I'm beginning to see the light on the God part, after what happened last spring. But seeing a glimmer and knowing what to do about it are two different things.

"Of course not." I gave Carly a look. "We all go together. And we walk, in case no one told you, so plan your shoes carefully."

"Oh, I will." She sat back on her hands, an "I *so* see right through you" smile turning up the corners of her mouth. "And it's all about the worship, I know." That smile told me she knew exactly what my motivation was. Part of it, at least. Hey, can you blame me?

The music changed and Danyel's voice lifted into a lonely blues melody, pouring over Carly's words like cream. I just melted right there on the spot. Man, could that boy sing.

> Blue water, blue sky
> Blue day, girl, do you think that I
> Don't see you, yeah I do.
> Long sunset, long road,
> Long life, girl, but I think you know
> What I need, yeah, you do.

I do a little singing my own self, so I know talent when I hear it. And I'd have bet you that month's allowance that Danyel had composed that one. He segued into the chorus and then the bridge, its rhythms straight out of Mississippi but the tune something new, something that fit the sadness and the hope of the words.

Wait a minute.

Blue day? Long sunset? Long road? As in, a long road to San Francisco?

Whoa. Could Danyel be trying to tell someone something? "You think that I don't see you"? Well, if that didn't describe *me*, I didn't know what would. Ohmigosh.

Could he be trying to tell me his feelings with a song? Musicians were like that. They couldn't tell a person something to her face, or they were too shy, or it was just too hard to get out, so they poured it into their music. For them, maybe it was easier to perform something than to get personal with it.

Be cool, girl. Let him finish. Then find a way to tell him you understand—and you want it, too.

The last of the notes blew away on the breeze, and a big comber smashed itself on the sand, making a sound like a kettle-drum to finish off the song. I clapped, and the others joined in.

"Did you write that yourself?" Lissa removed a marshmallow from her stick and passed it to him. "It was great."

Danyel shrugged one shoulder. "Tune's been bugging me for a while and the words just came to me. You know, like an IM or something."

Carly laughed, and Kaz's forehead wrinkled for a second in a frown before he did, too.

I love modesty in a man. With that kind of talent, you couldn't blame Danyel for thinking he was all that.

Should I say something? The breath backed up in my chest. *Say it. You'll lose the moment.* "So who's it about?" I blurted, then felt myself blush.

"Can't tell." His head was bent as he picked a handful of notes and turned them into a little melody. "Some girl, probably."

"Some girl who's leaving?" I said, trying for a teasing tone. "Is that a good-bye?"

"Could be."

I wished I had the guts to come out and ask if he'd written the song for me—for us—but I just couldn't. Not with everyone sitting there. With one look at Carly, whose eyes held a distinct "What's up with you?" expression, I lost my nerve and shut up. Which, as any of the girls could tell you, doesn't happen very often.

Danyel launched into another song—some praise thing that everyone knew but me. And then another, and then a cheesy old John Denver number that at least I knew the words to, and then a bunch of goofy songs half of us had learned at camp when we were kids. And then it was nearly midnight, and Kaz got up and stretched.

He's a tall guy. He stretches a long way. "I'm running the mixer for the early service tomorrow, so I've got to go."

Danyel got up, and I just stopped my silly self from saying, "No, not yet." Instead, I watched him sling the guitar over one shoulder and yank his board out of the sand. "Are you going to early service, too?" I asked him.

"Yeah," he said, sounding a little surprised. "I'm in the band, remember?"

Argh! As if I didn't know. As if I hadn't sat there three Sundays in a row, watching his hands move on the frets and the light make shadows under his cheekbones.

"I just meant—I see you at the late one when we go. I didn't know you went to both." Stutter, bumble. *Oh, just stop talking, girl. You've been perfectly comfortable talking to him so far. What's the matter?*

"I don't, usually. But tomorrow they're doing full band at early service, too. Last one before all the *turistas* go home. Next week we'll be back to normal." He smiled at me. "See you then."

Was he looking forward to seeing me, or was he just being nice? "I hope so," I managed.

"Kaz, you coming?"

Kaz bent to the fire and ran a stick through the coals, separating them. "Just let me put this out. Lissa, where's the bucket?"

"Here." While I'd been obsessing over Danyel, Lissa had run down to the waterline and filled a gallon pail. You could tell they'd done this about a million times. She poured the water on the fire and it blew a cloud of steam into the air. The orange coals gave it up with a hiss.

I looked up to say something to Danyel about it and saw that he was already fifty feet away, board under his arm like it weighed nothing, heading down the beach to the public lot where he usually parked his Jeep.

I stared down into the coals, wet and dying.

I couldn't let the night go out like this.

"Danyel, wait!" The sand polished the soles of my bare feet better than the pumice bar at the salon as I ran to catch up with him. A fast glance behind me told me Lissa had stepped up and begun talking to Kaz, giving me a few seconds alone.

I owed her, big time.

"What's up, ma?" He planted the board and set the guitar case down. "Forget something?"

"Yes," I blurted. "I forgot to tell you that I think you're amazing."

He blinked. "Whoa." The barest hint of a smile tickled the corners of his lips.

I might not get another chance as good as this one. I rushed on, the words crowding my mouth in their hurry to get out. "I know there's something going on here and we're all leaving on Tuesday and I need to know if you—if you feel the same way."

"About . . . ?"

"About me. As I feel about you."

He put both hands on his hips and gazed down at the sand. "Oh."

Cold engulfed me, as if I'd just plunged face-first into the dark waves twenty feet away. "Oh," I echoed. "Never mind. I guess I got it wrong." I stepped back. "Forget about it. No harm done."

"No, Shani, wait—"

But I didn't want to hear the "we can still be friends" speech. I didn't want to hear anything except the wind in my ears as I ran back to the safety of my friends.

KazG   It didn't work.

Dijon   Yo, Cyrano. You don't know that.

KazG   I know her. And it went right over her head. I can't believe you told everyone I IM'd the lyrics to you.

Dijon   They thought I was kidding, man.

KazG   Shani knows something. Check out all those questions.

Dijon   She was just making conversation.

KazG   What do I do now?

Dijon   I dunno. But your stand-in is off duty as of now. I'm sending Lissa a video to share with them. Want to go in on it with me?

KazG   Nah, I've gotta regroup. But Lissa will freak when she sees it.

Dijon   She's funny when she freaks. In a good way.

Delivered by Hand
September 21, 2009

His Serene Highness Sheikh Amir al-Aarez
Kingdom of Yasir
Office of the Private Secretary

Dr. Natalie Curzon, Principal
Spencer Academy
2600 Washington Street
San Francisco, California 94111

Dr. Curzon, greetings.

I am pleased to inform you that final security checks of the Spencer Academy campus have been completed. As outlined by our office earlier this summer, this letter will confirm His Serene Highness's requirements for the accommodation of his beloved son, Prince Rashid al Amir.

1. It is not acceptable that the heir to the Lion Throne should stay in anything other than a private room. Therefore, Mr. Travis Fanshaw must be removed to another room.
2. In view of the regrettable incident involving Lady Lindsay MacPhail of the United Kingdom last May, the Prince's personal security force will number not one agent, but two. One agent will be accommodated within the Prince's room itself. The other will sleep in an adjoining room. I trust the students will appreciate the privilege of supporting the safety of the heir and will not be too greatly discommoded.
3. If the Prince prefers not to take his lessons with the other students, male tutors will be provided for him.
4. The Prince will not under any circumstances disrobe in the presence of others. Therefore his participation in physical education classes will be limited to those that do not require a uniform or special clothing. Should it be his wish to participate, he will require private shower and toilet facilities.
5. The Prince's focus shall be on his studies. Please do your utmost to encourage him in academic endeavors, keeping always in mind that you are assisting in the education of a future king.

I am sure that Spencer Academy, its faculty, and its students are cognizant of the honor done their institution. I trust His Highness will enjoy a happy and productive term.

With very best wishes for your health, I remain,

Farshad Ma'mun

Farshad Ma'mun, MBA, Ph.D.
Private Secretary to His Serene Highness
The Sheikh of Yasir

chapter 2

NO WAY WAS I going by my single self to the early service at Lissa's church. One, I'd never hear the end of it, and two, I wasn't about to sit all by my little lonesome among the old folks, gawking hopelessly at Danyel and forgetting to sing.

So, I went with my girls at eleven and gawked and forgot to sing.

Honestly, who can sing when a man so fine is up there on that stage, his hair tied back so it makes a puff at the nape of his neck, wearing a white shirt that totally pops against his mocha skin? And don't get me started on his hands, moving on the neck of the guitar, pulling praise out of the strings with those long fingers.

Did I happen to mention that I go to church ninety percent to make my friends happy and ten percent for me? Maybe I'm hoping to get answers, even though I don't even know how to ask the questions. And maybe I like looking at the scenery. But before you go all squinty-eyed and write me off as a bobble-head, I know how to show respect. But it's hard to get into it the way Lissa and Gillian do, when the Lord hasn't paid much attention to me for the last, oh, seventeen years. I guess I go with them to see if He'll talk to me the way He seems to do for them.

Anyway, the sermon gave me some time to think. Specifically, about last night. No, not the Danyel part. The part that came later, when we girls were getting ready for bed.

After Carly and I had said good night to Lissa and her dad, and Carly had made her nightly call to her boyfriend, Brett—during which I sat out of earshot on the patio and admired the moonlight reflected in the swimming pool—she'd joined me.

"I miss him so much," she said as she slid into the lounge chair next to mine.

"I don't know how. You talk, like, five times a day, and send pictures and texts. It's the next best thing to being there."

"I'm not there, though." She sighed. "And it's hard to send a hug over e-mail."

"Cheer up. Only two more days and you're back in paradise."

"Easy for you, *chiquita*." She glanced sideways at me. "You're in paradise right now."

"You got that right." I slid down further on the lounger. "I'm seriously thinking of sleeping out here."

"There are bugs," she reminded me. "And you know that isn't what I meant."

"Yeah?"

"I know you're crushing on Danyel."

I scrambled up to a sitting position so I could stare at her. "How do you know that? Who told you? Did he say something?"

She shook her head at me, grinning. "Somebody goose you?"

"Don't mess me around, Carly. He didn't tell you that, did he?"

"Relax." She waved a lazy hand at me and I settled down. A little. "I was just watching you, is all. You think you're such a poker face and you're totally not. Every time I turn around, you're talking to him."

"Fat lot of good it does me." I slid down low on my spine. "He just wants to be friends. Him and Kaz, they're probably laughing at me right now."

"Why would they laugh?" Lissa padded up behind us, pulled the hems of her cotton pj bottoms over her knees, and sat on the edge of the pool to dunk her feet in the water. "They're our friends. Nobody's laughing."

"How do you know?" I demanded. "I made a big old fool of myself tonight."

She gave me a look over the tops of her skinny glasses. She must have taken her contacts out already. "I've got eyes. Four of 'em. Those two aren't like that. And what do you mean, a fool of yourself?"

"Oh, I just let him know I was crazed over him." Listen to me. A month at the beach and I'm starting to talk like the surfers. "But he just wants to be friends."

"Oh, man." Lissa reached up and touched my foot in sympathy. "Are you sure?"

"Pretty sure. I told him I thought there could be something between us and he was all, 'Oh.' Like I told him I had some contagious disease."

"Maybe you misunderstood," Carly said. "What happened then?"

"Nothing. I took off."

"Well, there you go." Carly shook her head at me. "You don't know for sure. You can still change his mind. Get him to see you differently."

"Listen to her." Lissa nodded toward Carly. "She's our resident expert in getting a guy's attention."

"Yeah, but I don't have any exploding buildings or stalkers handy," I said. "All I've got is me, and that ain't workin' out so far."

"That's all I had," Carly said. "Brett told me he noticed me a long time before the whole stalker thing with Mac. Before that party we went to at Callum's, even. Besides, a guy doesn't want to be with you because you're accessorized with exploding buildings. It'll be because you're cute and wear a mean stiletto and have a laugh that won't quit."

My friend. This is one of the reasons I love her to pieces.

"From your lips to his ears," I said.

But on Monday, as we all talked and laughed through a barbecue on the patio, where Danyel and Kaz tried to cook this massive fish Kaz's dad had caught out on the bay, and Lissa's mom arrived from L.A. at the last minute to save them, all I could think of was the distance I was about to put between me and him. And on Tuesday, when we all piled our luggage into the Mercedes GL450 and strapped Lissa's surfboard to the roof rack, I realized that the whole thing was hopeless.

Only one good thing happened. Danyel and Kaz stood in the driveway, shaded by big oak trees, when Lissa started the hugfest. She's known these guys most of her life, so she's allowed to hug them, but then Carly got into the act. She hugs puppies in the pet store, and random children, so this didn't surprise anyone. Still, I'm no dummy—I grabbed the opportunity before it got away. If those two could hug Danyel and Kaz with impunity, I was gonna jump right in.

And oh, my, I could just feel my dream coming true as Danyel hesitated for just the barest second before his arms went around me and mine slid around his back. I sort of flattened my bad self against his chest—only for a moment—and enjoyed it right to the max. He smelled sooooooo good. I think he dropped a kiss on my hair but I'm not sure, because he sort of handed me off to Kaz and turned to hug Ms. Sutter, aka Lissa's mom, who was going with their driver, Bruno, in the sedan with yet more of our luggage in it.

But I'd had my moment. Maybe it didn't mean a thing to him other than "see ya, 'bye," but it was something.

And it made the moment I'd dreaded, where we pulled out calling "'Byeeee," a little more bearable.

DORM, SWEET DORM. I don't know about the other girls, but Spencer Academy feels more like home than my mom and dad's house. Even the smell of it—furniture polish, running shoes, and freshly cut grass—is kind of comforting. It doesn't change. It's always there to greet you when you come back, even when you've been gone for months.

I'd taken it for granted I'd be in the same room as last year, so I got a jolt when we went to Admin to get our keys and found a herd of confused, arguing boys ahead of us.

"I don't get it," a guy called Michael, who'd been in my English class last year, said. He'd shaved his spiky neo-Mohawk off and was sporting a buzz cut. "You're telling me this Rashid kid gets two rooms? What's up with that?"

"You have nothing to complain about, Mr. Stockton," the clerk snapped. How many times had she answered that question today? "It doesn't affect you."

"It does so. I want to room with Dashiel Geary, like last year."

"I'm afraid all the arrangements in the boys' dorms have been shuffled since last year."

"Because of this bozo and his two rooms?" Michael threw out his arms and looked around for some support. "What about Travis? What's he going to do?"

"That's none of your business. Now, here is your key. I hope you and Mr. Stapleton will enjoy your year."

"I'm not rooming with that cheating pothead!" Michael shouted, but he got elbowed out of the way by the crowd behind him.

When we finally got to the counter, the clerk was grim and perspiring. "Name?"

"Mansfield," Lissa said.

She slapped a key into Lissa's hand. "You're with Chang, same as last year."

"That's a relief," Lissa murmured as she slid to the side to make room for me.

"Name?"

"Hanna."

She must have thought I said "Scalpel!" because she slapped the key into my palm as if it was one. "You're with Aragon."

"I am?" Happiness did a little spiral in my chest.

"Don't give me any static," the woman said. "Aragon!"

"Right here. Thanks. Ms. Webster, what about Lindsay MacPhail? She was my roommate last year."

"The exchange student? She's not on the roster. Why would she be? The exchange was only for a term."

"Just asking." Carly glanced at me as the three of us left the office and collected our bags outside in the corridor. "I guess she couldn't talk her parents into letting her come, after all."

"We'll still see her. She has to come." Lissa hefted her ginormous duffel and left the surfboard in the vestibule for the next trip. "David Nelson's trial is set for October. Don't both of you have to testify?"

Carly nodded, her eyes pinching at the corners the way they do when she's worried. "Don't remind me. I'm not looking forward to it."

"Don't think about that now," I said. "We're roomies. We're seniors. There's *crème brulée* for dessert. Life is good."

"You're right." Carly shot me a smile as we climbed the stairs. "I feel older and smarter already."

"I am smarter," Lissa put in. "I'm taking bonehead chemistry this term and totally skating through everything else."

"Skating?" I waited for them on the second-floor landing. "Aren't you taking honors classes?"

"Well, yeah. English and Spanish. Oh, and I'm doing a capstone project in English. That's still skating."

"And you have to write the essay for the Hearst Prize," a new voice called, quick footsteps slapping on the stairs behind us. "That's more like a triple Axel."

"Gillian!"

We dumped our stuff all over the stairs and stampeded to meet her. Our whoops and greetings echoed in the dignified Edwardian reception hall, but none of us gave a rip. Ms. Tobin, our dorm mistress and the only person in school who cared about noise demerits, wasn't on duty until tomorrow.

"When did you get here? Why didn't you call me?" Lissa demanded, grabbing her around the waist and hugging her.

"Just now. I heard you guys yakking it up on the stairs when I came in at the front. I haven't even got my key."

"I've got mine. We're sharing together this year, too."

"Woo-hoo!" Gillian's bear hug practically knocked the air out of my lungs before she let me go. "I'm glad to see you, girl-friend. Nai-Nai sends her love, not to mention a box of pork buns. She's going to overnight them."

My stomach growled in appreciation. "I love that woman."

Gillian hugged Carly and then checked her out. "You did something to your hair."

Carly shook her head. "Nope. It was a week on the beach at Lissa's. I got natural highlights."

"She's in looooooove," I said. "It's that contented glow."

"Shut up," Carly said with affection, and bumped me with one hip.

"So where is the man?" Gillian looked around as if Brett would materialize out of the air. "I can't believe he isn't here to welcome you back."

Lissa heaved her bag onto her shoulder and gazed down the corridor toward her and Gillian's room as if it were a mile long. With that duffel, it would probably feel like it. "After fifty-seven text messages and a mile-by-mile replay all the way up the coast, there's nothing left to say."

"Just one thing." Carly picked up her own bags, and she and I prepared to hike up one more floor. "I have to tell him whether I'm coming for dinner at his house tonight."

"Like that needs an answer?" Gillian said with faux amazement.

"I wanted to see if you guys were doing anything first." Carly's tone was soft, almost shy. "After all, I didn't get to see much of you this summer."

I could have hugged her. In fact, I dropped my bag and did. "You are the best friend ever." Color flooded her cheeks.

"And the answer is, of course you should have dinner with Brett," Gillian told her. "You haven't seen him in what, a couple of weeks?"

Carly nodded.

"I know how I'd feel," Lissa put in.

"You'd dump us like a bunch of hot potstickers." Gillian grinned at her.

"Hey! I would not."

But all of us knew that she had, back when she'd dated what some people considered the hottest guy in school, Callum McCloud. And Gillian was a case of the potsticker calling the kettle black, because she'd done the same thing with Lucas Hayes.

But in my opinion, both of them would think twice now about ditching their girlfriends when a guy said, "Jump." They'd learned the hard way: Guys might come and guys might go, but your girlfriends are forever.

....

✉

To: shanna@spenceracad.edu
From: beryl.hanna@petronova.com
Date: September 22, 2009
Re: Hello from Cairo

Hey sweet thing, how are you? We have a 12-hour layover in Cairo before our flight to London, so I'm crashed on a big bed in the Four Seasons and catching up on e-mail. I'm thinking you should be back at school today, right? It's so hard to believe you're a senior. It seems like just last week we drove up that gravel drive, and you stood at the bottom of the stairs, trying to put on your game face before you went in. And now, soon you'll be buying a prom dress! Too bad the trip to Paris is *after* graduation. Though I must say I have a certain little plan for the spring couture shows ::zips lips::

I wanted to give you a heads-up about an old friend of yours. Remember when you were little and we went to Greece in the summer? You must've been six or so when we started going. Anyway, we always stayed in a white house that looked like a stack of sugar cubes, right on the beach, that belonged to some friends of ours. Back then they were just Zuleikha and Amir al-Aarez, but now they're Their Serene Highnesses of Yasir. And guess what? Their son Rashid is going to be doing an exchange term right there at Spencer!

We have an even closer connection with the family, did you know that? Besides a bunch of history I won't go into, your great-grandma Hanna married one of his uncles. It's not like you're related all that close, though—in case, you know, you wanted to date him! LOL.

Daddy says the prince did a couple of years in school in Switzerland before he decided to go to London. Now he's in San Francisco because he wants to take computer courses. He has his pick of all the schools in the world and he wants an M.B.A. from little old Stanford! I send Zuleikha your school picture every year, so at least he'll know what you look like. Have you met him yet? What's he like? I know you'll make him feel welcome, because he won't know a soul.

Daddy says the champagne is here. Must go.

Love you,
Mama

chapter 3

N THE DINING ROOM, Lissa, Gillian, and I made our entrance. Potent, wise, and reverend seniors, that was us, and we had the look to prove it. Lissa had French-braided her hair down both sides of her head and combined the two into one at her nape. With a floaty BCBG sundress, she looked like a model in a medieval photo shoot. Gillian had given up trying to tame her hair, so she'd focused on clothes—an antique burned-out velvet camisole and black capris with knock-you-out Balenciaga halter sandals.

And me? Let's just say that I hadn't wasted my three days in New York with the Changs before we'd gone to the Hamptons. Gillian and I had hit the trifecta—Bendel's, Bloomie's, and Barney's—and I sashayed into the dining room in a hot tangerine Carolina Herrera silk shift that screamed, "Look at me!"

The only thing better than making an entrance by yourself is making one with your friends. The problem was, our entrance barely registered.

The dining room was about three-quarters full of people who had already arrived. More would come tonight, and of course the day students would all be in class tomorrow. But even from the door, I could feel the buzz in the room.

"What's going on?" Lissa murmured.

"There's Jeremy." Gillian nodded toward her man, who waved and indicated he was saving the table for us. "He'll have the scoop."

We got our food—gourmet deep-dish pizza—and hurried to join him. He stood when Gillian put her plate next to his, and right in front of us all, slid an arm around her waist and kissed her.

Whoa. Gillian got all flustered and plunked into her chair as if her knees had failed. She bowed her head, and I realized it wasn't because of that. Everyone but me was saying grace.

After a few moments, Lissa lifted her head and got back on topic. "You know Tobin dishes demerits for PDAs."

"I couldn't help it." Hmph. He might be Mr. Romance, but look, the guy had made himself blush. "I haven't seen her for six weeks."

Gillian, still beet red, took a big bite of pizza.

"So, on the subject of making a sensation, what's going on here?" I asked. "I feel weirdness in the room."

"Check it." Jeremy gave a Gillian-like nod to his left. I followed his glance to see nothing but a group of guys sitting at the table next to the one claimed by Vanessa Talbot and her posse of A-listers. Two of the guys were in suits, facing the door.

Suits? That wouldn't cause the furtive glances and whispered conversations all around us. I exchanged glances with Gillian and Lissa. "So? They're a little overdressed, but—"

"Not the suits." Jeremy swallowed. "The other kid. The one in the white shirt."

"I can't see anything but the back of his head." And craning to look would be so not cool.

"That's who everyone's talking about. That's the prince."

"The what?" Lissa dropped her fork and it clattered on her china plate.

"Shhhhh!" I grabbed her elbow and forced myself to not stand up and gawk. "You've never seen a prince before?"

"Sure, but not in this dining room."

Since I'd been mostly kidding, I stopped. "What?"

"In Scotland, remember? The royal family went to church in one of the towns Dad was filming in. Wills and Harry were there. And yes," she said before I could ask, "they are both just as gorgeous in person as they are in *People*."

Okay, moment to recover. I mean, when you think that I'm sort of friends with the daughter of an earl, I guess having a friend who hobnobs with princes isn't so surprising. That was part of why my parents had been so enthused about my coming to Spencer. Stuff like this was pretty much routine around here. And then again, from what my mom had said in her e-mail, I knew this one myself. Or used to, when we were both so little that princes only existed in the pages of our storybooks.

"So, staying on topic," Gillian said, obviously having recovered her powers of speech, "the prince of what? Please tell me he's not related to Vanessa in any way."

"Not that I know of. He's from the Middle East. The Kingdom of Yasir." Blank looks. Jeremy nodded. "Right. I'd never heard of it, either. Someplace near Saudi Arabia, sitting on oil fields that make Saudi look low-rent. He's supposed to be worth a couple of billion all by himself."

I couldn't resist sneaking another peek. Huh. The little boy I'd dunked in the clear blue waves of the Med?

"And he's gracing us with his presence, why?" Lissa wanted to know. "Is he another exchange student?"

Jeremy nodded. "Channel Four did a segment on him on the weekend. Did you catch it?"

"Nope. We came up from Santa Barbara this morning. He's not news down there."

"So much for keeping a low profile," Gillian commented. "Not like Mac." None of us knew then that the British Embassy had had someone keeping an eye on her while she was here. Not that it had done any good when that nutjob David Nelson had kidnapped her.

"Yeah, his bodyguards are right up front," I mused, savoring my pizza. "But I guess if you call a press conference and tell everyone you're here, you're not very interested in a low profile, are you? It's just more props for the school. I bet Curzon's ecstatic."

Like most of the people in the room, I kept half an eye on the prince while I finished my pizza and made a trip to the dessert bar afterward to bag a *crème brulée*. Too bad he had his back to the room. All I could see was dark hair, perfectly cut, and a bit of tanned neck. I wanted to see how he'd turned out now that he was all grown up. I wanted to see if he'd recognize me. Then I shook my head at my bad self.

Never mind scoping out the prince, you hound. You left your heart in Santa Barbara, remember?

"Guess we won't be hangin' with the prince, will we?" I asked Lissa in a low voice when I came back to the table. Gillian and Jeremy were still at the dessert bar. There was no way he'd remember me, or that I'd tell anyone we'd once played together. And if he didn't, that was cool, too. It wasn't like his life had anything to do with mine now. One more thing to let slide away on good-bye.

"Why would we want to?" she asked. "That's Vanessa's department. Ten to one, if she were here, she'd be all over him. I bet she'd even invite him to sit at the sacred table."

"He might be nice."

"I'm sure he is. But you can't find out unless you go over and talk to him. You're welcome to go first."

I snorted into my soda. "Yeah, right. 'So, Your Highness, what's shakin'? Wanna hang?'"

She snickered. "Go on. I dare you."

"I'd have to get past the bodyguards first. Fill out an application for an audience. Wait six weeks for it to be approved. Get the invitation—engraved, of course. Make an appointment. And by that time, the term will be over and he'll be flying off home in his private Concorde before I even got to say a word."

Lissa hid behind her soda, trying not to laugh out loud.

"What are you two giggling about?" Gillian whispered as she came back with her dessert.

"Nothing," I managed, glancing over at the prince's table again. One of his bodyguards got up. "Ooh. Hey," I whispered. "Clear the area. His Highness is getting dessert."

Lissa lost it and leaned on one arm as she pushed me with the other hand.

The bodyguard walked slowly across the dining room, his impassive face scanning this way and that. He moved with an eerie smoothness, like a droid with well-greased ball bearings for joints. One hand rested at his hip, where I'd bet my bank account he had, if not a pistol of some kind, then at least a stun gun. The other hand tapped the side of his head briefly, where a curly wire like a fine phone cord ran up out of his jacket and into a transmitter in his ear.

So Secret Service.

All this fuss to get the guy his dessert? Did they reconnoiter the stalls when they took him to the bathroom, too? I shook my head and drained the last of my soda. When I put the can down, I jumped about four feet.

Secret Service Guy stood right behind me. "Miss Hanna?"

I stared at him so long that Lissa finally had to nudge me with her elbow. "Huh? Are you talking to me?"

"You are Miss Shani Hanna?"

"Uh, yeah." *What's it to you?* I bit back the words. It's not very smart to say stuff like that to people carrying unidentified weapons.

"Would you please come with me?" His accent was a combination of British and the accent I'd heard on news reports where the Middle East reps to the U.N. are talking.

"I don't think so," I said.

"Please, miss. His Royal Highness wishes to speak with you."

Beside me, Lissa made a choking sound. Gillian and Jeremy stared, their gazes bouncing from me to Secret Service Guy like they were watching a tennis match.

"What?" I blurted. Was I dreaming? That was it. We were still on the highway. I'd fallen asleep in the car and the whole evening—arrival, dinner, my tangerine dress—was a figment of my imagination.

"His Royal Highness wishes to speak to you," the man repeated. Slowly.

Lissa's elbow connected with my ribs this time, hard. "Uh, why?" A legitimate question, right?

"I do not question His Royal Highness, miss. I am to escort you to his table. That is all."

I gave one second's thought to saying, "Dude, if that's all he wants, he can come over here and say hey like a normal person." But I didn't.

Instead, I got up and hoped I wouldn't do anything stupid like fall off my Jimmy Choos while I made the long, long walk to the table next to the window.

The whole dining room had gone as silent as a final exam. Tap. Tap. My heels sounded like castanets. Or like that drum you hear in movies when people get marched up to the guillotine.

I lifted my chin. Well, I hadn't worn a tangerine Herrera because I wanted to hide behind the potted palms. If you had to meet a prince you hadn't spared one thought for in a dozen years, you couldn't do much better.

We stopped behind him. Secret Service Guy cleared his throat. And the prince turned.

Wow to the tenth power.

Dark eyes. Deeply tanned skin and a hawklike nose. Sharp cheekbones narrowing to a chin that meant business. A nicely cut mouth and a soul patch.

I barely remembered my little companion from the Greek beach. There was nothing familiar in this face at all—but, my oh my, there was certainly nothing wrong with it.

He stood, and I tilted my head up. Even though I had on stiletto heels, he still topped me by a good four inches.

"Your Royal Highness," Secret Service Guy said, "may I present Miss Shani Hanna. Miss Hanna, His Royal Highness Prince Rashid al Amir, heir to the Lion Throne of Yasir."

Long-ago playmate or not, I knew exactly what to do. I hadn't watched a hundred historical DVDs with Carly for nothing. Not to mention gone obediently to the etiquette module every week in freshman Life Sciences. I extended my hand as if I were conferring a knighthood, and he took it as I sank into a curtsy that would have made even Mac's mom, the Countess of Strathcairn, proud.

A gentle tug brought me to my feet again and he looked down into my eyes. He didn't let go of my hand. "A very great pleasure, Miss Hanna," he said in a voice like midnight, rough with stars. "I feel as if I have been waiting an eternity to see you again. Do you remember me?"

His eyes were a brown so deep, they looked black, and authority and appreciation sparkled in them. I opened my mouth to say something gracious. Something memorable. Something he and the hundred and fifty eavesdroppers all around us would remember and talk about for weeks to come.

"Do you still skinny-dip in the ocean?" I asked.

"JUST SHOOT ME now."

I fell face down on the bed and pulled my goosedown pillow over my head to shut out the world and the aftereffects of my own idiocy. The bed dipped as Carly sat next to me and pulled the pillow away.

"Get over yourself, *chiquita*." I could hear the giggle in her voice, even if she was too nice to really let it go. "You were little kids."

"Go ahead. Laugh. I know you want to."

She toppled over, too, arms wrapped around the pillow, giggling at the ceiling. "I can't believe you said that to him."

"I'm never getting over this. Never. He's going to think I'm a complete fool."

"No, he won't. He sure knows you remember him now, though."

"You just can't say anything that personal to a future king. Off with my head!"

Someone knocked on the door and pushed it open. "Is this the Department of Deportment?" Lissa asked in an oh-so-bright tone. "I need a curtsy lesson, please. Or is that next door in the Department of Dweebery?"

"Now it starts," I said to the ceiling.

"Where'd you learn to do that?" Gillian crowded in behind her. "It looked really good."

"Everybody learns it in freshman etiquette." I rolled over as they draped themselves on the furniture, which in our case was limited to two beds and two desks with ergonomic chairs. "Along with which fork to use, how to address a head of state, and how not to embarrass yourself in front of a room full of people."

"Failed that one, I bet." Lissa rooted in the fridge and started tossing out Odwallas.

I caught a strawberry lemonade and cracked the cap. "I'd have paid more attention if I'd thought I was going to actually use anything in that module."

"You did, though," Carly pointed out. "Last June, remember, when I got that award? You told me what to say to the mayor. And then he asked me to call him Gavin anyway."

"But you didn't have to curtsy to him."

"True," Carly acknowledged. "But I know who to come to if I ever have to meet Mac's parents."

"You could ask Mac," Gillian said. "I'd buy a ticket to watch her curtsy to anyone."

"I wish we *could* ask Mac," Carly said. "I never thought I'd say this, but I miss her. She's really solid under all the fireworks and attitude."

"She wouldn't have said anything stupid to Rashid," I put in. "She'd reduce the Secret Service to ash in one second and have him groveling at her feet, begging her to let him buy her a Caribbean island in the next."

They all laughed, and Lissa gave me a sideways glance. "So how come you never told us you used to know him?"

"It never came up. And I forgot he existed until my mom told me about him in an e-mail." I willed the blush back down to where it came from.

"It is a little weird, though," Gillian said. "His singling you out of the crowd like that."

"Not to mention recognizing you when you didn't recognize him," Carly added.

"He was just dazzled by my beauty, and Vanessa wasn't there to upstage me." I congratulated my clever self on my airy tone.

"But it's no big mystery. My mom sends his mom my school picture every year. Maybe she showed one to him."

They seemed to accept that, and then they pounced on Gillian, demanding the scoop on her love life. I lay on my back, my gaze on the plaster border of Greek keys on the ceiling and my mind on a pair of dark eyes.

Make that two pairs. Both brown, both full of intelligence and humor and the knowledge of the power they had over girls.

Just yesterday, I'd wanted with all my heart for Danyel Johnstone to look at me as though I were his dream come to life.

But he hadn't. The prince had.

And what was I going to do about *that*, I'd like to know?

chapter 4

ATER IN THE EVENING, the girls dragged me to Room 216 for the first prayer circle of senior year. You're probably wondering why I went when I was so sketchy on the subject of religion. But the truth was, I kind of liked it. It reminded me of my grandma in a weird way, even though she's been singing alto in heaven for five years now. It felt safe to be there, and it reminded me of my promise to myself that I wouldn't be an island anymore.

After we cleaned out the room (who were they going to get to do this when we weren't around next year?), we dragged in chairs from classrooms they'd migrated to. We still had a couple of minutes to go before seven, and Jeremy wasn't there yet, so Gillian amused herself at the little spinet while we waited.

Gillian, in case you didn't know, is at Spencer on a music scholarship. She's not only brilliant at science and math, but she's a concert pianist who never gives concerts. Oh, she practices in the music rooms because that's what music students do, but the girl could fill the auditorium downtown at the Opera House if she wanted. She and Yo-Yo Ma, tearing it up. I could see it now.

So when I say she was amusing herself, it was with some

dead German guy's concerto that involved fingers moving so fast they blurred as they executed intricate runs up and down the keyboard. How she remembers all those notes is a mystery. Probably the same way she remembers chemical formulas and how to start Pascal's triangle. As Carly would say, it's a gift.

The door opened and Jeremy came in, looking over his shoulder as he held the door. I smiled at him and then turned to see who else was with him. Usually it's just us the Tuesday night before term starts, because Gillian doesn't go around putting up her signs until later in the week, so I wasn't expecting anyone else.

Which is why, when Lady Lindsay MacPhail walked into the room, sheer disbelief froze my smiling lips to my teeth.

Gillian lost her place in the concerto and came to a crashing halt. Carly said something really high and loud in Spanish and flung herself at Mac. At which point everyone started talking at once.

"I can't believe it! What are you doing here?"

"This is prayer circle, right?"

"Mac, you look amazing. Tell me that's not a Dior."

"Gillian, you got your hair cut!"

"Dude, do these chicks always tweak like this?"

Carly dragged Mac over to a chair, so the rest of us followed to hear what miracle had brought her back. I grinned at the sound of her accent, plummy and posh with just an edge of a burr on her r's. I suppose you can take the girl out of Scotland, but you can't take Scotland out of the girl.

"Tell all," Carly demanded. "Now, before I split a seam."

"I never thought I'd say this, but I'm glad to see you all again," Mac said. "Mummy and Dad fought it every step of the way, because I'm supposed to be prepping for Oxford, but I asked them, what makes you think I'm going to uni in the U.K.? What if I want to go to Harvard?"

"You do?" Gillian asked. "I didn't know that."

"I don't, but what if I did?" Mac retorted. "I might want to go to Stanford or Princeton or any number of places, and all they can see is stuffy old Oxford because both of them went there. And then there was the David situation. If you don't think I made the most of *that*, think again," she said with a dangerous smile, tossing her red curls over one shoulder. "In the end, since I have to come back for the trial and probably for a—what do you call it? An appeal?" She looked at Gillian, resident *CSI* expert, who nodded. "They finally concluded I might as well come over for the term. Mummy promised she'd come for the trial, too, for moral support."

"What about your dad?" I asked.

Mac leaned forward a little. "Just my opinion, of course," she said, "but I don't think he can bear to see David. He never has, you know. He's being typically Dad and hiding from anything that's unpleasant." She snorted and sat back. "Like it'll go away."

"Well, I'm going to pray for him," Gillian told her. "Come on, everyone. Let's get started."

Mac shook her head. "I'm not the praying sort. You can pass me by. I just came to find you all since Carly wasn't in her room."

Gillian and Lissa exchanged a smile, as if they knew something the rest of us didn't. I couldn't imagine what, but if Mac could speak up, so could I.

"Me, too," I said. "Not the praying kind, I mean." I paused and looked into my friends' faces. "For now."

"Cool." Carly gave me a big grin.

"Wait a second." Gillian looked at Mac. "How'd you know Carly wasn't in her room?"

"I went in and had a look 'round, obviously," Mac said.

I tried to puzzle this out. "You have a key to our room?"

"Oh, were those your things? I thought those orange Dolce & Gabbana pumps looked familiar. The dorms seem to be very crowded this term, and since I came in at the last minute, pulling strings all the way, they've put me in with you."

"Cool squared!" Carly gave this idea the thumbs-up.

I felt like leaping to my feet and heading for the Admin office at a dead run, howling "No!" every step of the way. Since when did they put three people in a room designed for two? Especially when one was Mac, who took up more than the usual person's amount of space.

"Isn't that going to be a little tight?" I asked, keeping it light and friendly. "I mean, I know how much you travel with."

"That was before, when I didn't know what to expect. I didn't bring my motorbike helmet this time, for instance, since the likelihood of being invited to one of Brett's wineries is fairly low."

"I wouldn't put money on that," Lissa said with a glance at Carly.

"So I ditched all the suitcases and just came with two trunks. They're vintage—Dad's had them in the attic with all the other clobber from the last couple of centuries. They function like closets when they have to."

"And I'm happy to share my wardrobe with you," Carly told her. "My side of the bathroom cabinet, too."

Okay, this was making me sound like I resented her being there and I was some kind of space hog to boot. Both were the last impressions I wanted to give.

"We'll all share," I said with a big smile. "It'll be fun."

Then, to my relief, Gillian called us to order a second time and they got down to the serious business of praying. When Lissa's turn came, she gave us a big grin and pulled her Mac-Book out from under her chair. She flipped it open and pressed Play on a movie that was cued up on the screen.

The video started and the first thing I saw was a close-up of Danyel's face. I realized my jaw was hanging open and I shut it with a snap. How soon could I get a copy of that video? Then I realized what I was looking at: He'd joined us *au virtuel* at prayer circle.

"Lord, thanks for bringing all my friends safe back to school without running into anything or the cars stalling out on the hills. I hope You'll bless them while they hang together at Your feet to pray. Be with my buddy Kaz, because he's pretty disturbed these days." He took a deep breath. "Be with my friend Lissa and give her strength to deal with . . . stuff, and I hope we'll feel Your presence with us as we go to classes and start the new term. I pray you'll work in Mac's heart and Shani's too, because wow, Father, I can't imagine getting through a day all by myself. Help them to come to know You. In the name of my big brother Jesus, amen."

I was so stunned about somebody addressing the Big Guy on my behalf, that Lissa had closed the notebook and begun praying before I could even react.

"Father God, thank You for all my friends who walk beside me while Your angels have my back. Thank You for bringing Danyel here via e-mail, and Mac via British Airways. I know You want me to learn the power of discernment, Lord. I really need it when I deal with my parents. I don't know what's going on there, but when You tell me, I hope You'll give me the strength to do whatever I need to. Maybe You could put it in my mom's heart to stay around home a little more. She says it's fund-raising for a good cause, but it can't be so good when my dad's so unhappy. I pray for Your spirit on them, Father, and on me, especially when I'm around Vanessa Talbot. Amen."

Whoa. Lissa's parents were having troubles? Yuck. That couldn't be good. I wasn't really sure about this prayer thing, but I sent up a silent request to the Big Guy that they'd work it out. Not that I knew whole bunches about parents working things out. I assumed mine did, because they always seemed normal when they were around me, and extended absences were just part of who they were. I'd gotten over wishing they'd stick around and be a family with me years ago.

Maybe that was why I was so determined to be the perfect

friend with the people in this room. They were my family now. They seemed to like having me around, and with the possible teensy exception of Mac, I felt the same about them. But Carly liked Mac, and I liked Carly, so for her sake, I'd try.

To: lmansfield@spenceracad.edu
From: kazg@hotmail.com
Date: September 25, 2009
Re: Auugghhh

I hope you know how much life stinks right now. I really need my best bud and where are you? Frolicking in the fog without me. Even catching some good waves after school today didn't help. Dan was with me, but that empty space on the invisible board on my other side just made me miss you more.

I know you've got parental problems and yeah, I'd be worried too. Absence does not make the heart grow fonder. It just makes the heart forget what it liked about the other person. Not that I'm forgetting you, girl. It's different with parents, I guess.

In other news, it's been four months and counting since that publisher got my manuscript for DEMON BATTLE. I bet it's holding open the mailroom door. I bet no one's going to read it because it does a better job with the door than it does at entertaining anybody.

Aw, delete this message. I need to go give my head a shake. Pray for me, wouldja?

(((hug)))
Kaz

chapter 5

I NEVER PAID MUCH ATTENTION to classes before last year. Like I said, they were just something to get through with the highest grades possible on my way to bigger and better things. But, you know, hanging out with Gillian Chang changes your ideas.

That girl loves learning stuff. Doesn't matter whether it's calculus or the best way to letter thought-bubbles on a graphic panel—she's into it.

Carly, too. On Friday she scampered off to her Fashion Design module like it was Christmas and all the presents under the tree were for her. Of course, since she carried off first prize at Design Your Dreams last June, the presents probably *are* for her. It's not every day Stella McCartney offers you an internship in London for the summer.

It's not every day Stella gets turned down.

Nicely, of course. I can't imagine Carly being anything but nice about it. But she feels a lot of loyalty to Tori Wu, who has a loft in Chinatown and who designs these amazing dresses, and plus she was going to get paid, and *plus* she could still see her family on weekends, so it was a no-brainer to stay stateside and get some fabu training—not to mention swag.

And did I tell you about the e-mail she got on Monday, before we left for the opening assembly?

✉

To: CAragon@spenceracad.edu
From: OWebster@spenceracad.edu
Date: September 28, 2009
Re: Senior Life Sciences requirement

Miss Aragon,

In view of your success at the Design Your Dreams event hosted by Spencer Academy last June, and with the glowing reports we have received from Ms. Tori Wu concerning your performance as an intern with her fashion house, I am pleased to tell you that your senior Life Sciences requirement has been waived.

Instead, I am offering you the position of teacher's assistant. For your help each Friday in the Fashion Design classes, you will receive a monthly stipend and your grade will be transferred to your Work Experience credit, which will of course make you a competitive candidate on your college applications. You will also have unlimited personal use of the Fashion Design resources and equipment, should you choose to use them.

Congratulations on your achievements, and I look forward to your contributions this year.

Orland Webster, M.Ed.
Dean of Students
Spencer Academy

Brett Loyola noticed the glow on Carly's face as soon as he located her in the crowd in the assembly hall—aka the ballroom—and came to sit with us. The guys from the rowing team sat behind and around us, including some guy with serious shoulders who got comfortable between Gillian and Lissa. Which wouldn't make Jeremy happy when he got there. *That's what you get for being late, my friend.*

"What's up?" Brett said to Carly. Even I could tell that he thought she was the best thing since music on a chip, the way he looked down into her face. They'd been a couple since the night Mac was kidnapped last May. I mean, that situation pretty much redlined what Brett called the weird-o-meter, but what was even more amazing to me was that he hadn't lost interest a month later and moved on.

Don't get me wrong—that wasn't a slam. She's my friend and I love her, but, well, she's Carly, the Latina scholarship kid. Not Vanessa Talbot or Dani Lavigne or any of the glossy posse who have hung on Brett's arm ever since his voice changed. She's an ordinary girl with, okay, a little more talent and sweetness than most, and she'd accomplished what many women before her had not.

She'd made Brett care.

Their heads tilted close together as she told him the happy news, and heads turned and texts flew as he hugged her and gave her a big kiss on the lips in front of everybody within three rows.

Lucky for them, Ms. Tobin and Mr. Milsom, the terrors of the dormitories, were busy with a bunch of confused freshmen at the door and missed the show. I glanced at Lissa and smiled. The corners of her mouth twitched up and fell, and she looked past me at the lovebirds, whispering away in their own little world.

Her face turned bleak.

"Are you okay?"

"Define 'okay.'"

"The absence of disease, disaster, or midterms."

"Then I'm okay."

That still left a huge list of stuff that could be wrong. Ms. Curzon, the headmistress, walked up to the microphone and her image appeared on the projection screens above the stage. I couldn't say any more, but I promised myself I'd get with Gillian and find out what was going on with Lissa. If it was just her family, there wasn't much I could do but be sympathetic and supportive and sneak her chocolate between classes. If there was something else going on with her, then it was our job to help.

I mean, even we non-Christians can figure out that much.

"Good morning, everyone," Ms. Curzon began in her half-American, half-British accent. "Welcome to your first full week at Spencer Academy, and for some of you, may I say, welcome to your first term. I look forward to another class of students learning what our school colors stand for: loyalty, purity, and intellect."

A video produced by the media classes began to play on the screen, but since it involved rah-rah stuff like the sports teams and winning and all the exciting extracurriculars you could sign up for, I tuned out and admired the workmanship in my Louboutin pumps instead. Since all of us wore the same uniforms, the only place you could get creative during class hours was with hair and shoes. And, as the girls will tell you, I do the most with both.

Gillian slid out of her chair and made her way unobtrusively up the side aisle. I tuned back in and elbowed Lissa. "Where's she going?" Lissa shook her head as Gillian paused next to the ficus forest that concealed the staircase up to the stage.

"Seniors, your plates will be full this term," Ms. Curzon

went on, and reluctantly I turned my attention back to her. "Not only do you have college applications—and may I remind you that the university acceptance rate of Spencer students is ninety-eight percent—but don't forget your Community Service requirement. If you don't have twenty credits by June, you won't graduate, so make it a point to visit the counseling office sometime before the holiday break to decide on ways in which you may serve.

"Now, it gives me great pleasure to introduce one of our music students, senior Gillian Chang, who will perform Richard Strauss's *Also Sprach Zarathustra*."

Gillian bounded up the stairs while everyone applauded, and seated herself at the huge antique Steinway on the far side. Within a few bars, even the ignorant mopes who'd been rude enough to chatter during announcements had fallen silent, watching her slender body throw itself into the chords and the emotional buildup of the theme.

She wasn't amusing herself now. That girl could seriously play.

And when she was done, you could hear a paperclip drop in the big ballroom. Lissa and I looked at each other, and we leaped to our feet, clapping as hard as we could. Our whole row did likewise, and of course when the rowing team got into it, everyone decided a standing ovation was the thing to do.

Gillian grinned as she ran down the steps and came back to her seat on a wave of congratulations and praise. You could barely hear Ms. Curzon dismiss us all, and it was a good thing we didn't have to do something as anticlimactic as go to class. Instead, we went straight to an early lunch.

Brett and his buds from the rowing team dragged two tables together so we could all sit in a big, noisy bunch. "How lovely," Mac purred to me as we loaded our plates.

"What, the fish and chips make you feel at home?" Of course, we weren't talking about limp fries wrapped in newspaper. At Spencer this meant Alaskan halibut in light-as-air tempura batter, with hand-cut potatoes and a tomato-basil salad.

"No," she said. "I meant the male-to-female ratio at our table. Much improved since last year, I'd say."

I'd say so, too. There was totally an advantage to having connections with the team captain. "You won't see me complaining." We grinned at each other and returned to our seats. I have to admit, the accord between us on this subject, at least, felt pretty good.

Except someone had moved her blue school cardigan from the chair next to mine and made himself comfortable while his servants—er, agents—got his lunch.

"Your Highness," I said a little awkwardly. "How, um, nice of you to join us." *Even though you weren't invited.*

Then I gave myself a mental smack. I was the only person he knew here. Of course he'd want to sit with me. Us.

"It is my pleasure." I hoped we wouldn't have to watch our mouths and use our forks to eat our fries.

"Hello," Mac said on his other side as she slid into the seat marked with her cardigan.

"Lady Lindsay," the prince said solemnly.

"Oh, please." She picked up a fry with her fingers, dipped it in ranch dressing, and waved it back and forth like a shaking head. "Don't call me that. My name is Mac." Then she popped the fry in her mouth.

Okay. If she could, then I could. "So how about it, Your Highness? First-name basis here?"

His smile could light ships into harbor, it was so perfectly white. "Of course. You both must call me Rashid."

One of the agents set his plate in front of him and spread a napkin on his knee. I waited until he stepped back to stand against the wall behind us. "Will your bodyguards get bent out of shape about it?"

"It is not for them to say." He glanced at Mac's plate, and she pushed the dish of ranch dressing closer to him. He picked up a fry with his fingers and, instead of taking the invitation, he dipped it into my ketchup instead. Uh, okay. Maybe he didn't know what the bottles on the condiment bar were for. "My father would prefer that no one forget the proprieties, but my father is on the other side of the world." He paused. "This is very good. What is the white mixture you are eating?"

"A lovely American thing called ranch dressing. But you should try your chips with salt and vinegar when they have hamburgers on Fridays," Mac suggested. "You'll never go back."

The agent was back at his elbow, speaking a language I didn't know. Rashid answered him in the same language, only a lot briefer. Deliberately, he dipped another fry in my ketchup.

"My bodyguard objects to my sharing a dish with you," he informed me.

"I've got no known diseases, if that's what he's worried about."

"It's not that. It's an intimacy usually reserved for couples." He smiled into my eyes and I swallowed a half-chewed chunk of halibut sideways, choked, then grabbed my soda and gulped.

"Is that all it takes?" The guy with the shoulders from the rowing team dipped a fry in Gillian's ketchup and grinned at her, which made Jeremy flush and glare at him from under knitted brows.

"Not happening, Tate, my man," Brett said. "You need to do more than that to get Gillian's attention."

"Yeah, like have half a brain," Jeremy muttered. Fortunately, I don't think Tate heard him.

"You're some piano player," Tate told her. "I've never heard anything like it."

"Thanks." Calmly, she pushed her ketchup toward Jeremy, dipped one of her own fries, and offered it to him. Jeremy took it and, I swear, fell another fathom deep in love with her.

Brett grinned at his friend, who sat back with a shrug. Clearly he could take a hint without getting bent about it. Meanwhile, that left me with a prince cleaning up my ketchup. "You keep that up and it'll all be gone."

He turned and signaled to one of the bodyguards.

"Oh, please." I got up. "I'll get my own."

"No, no. It is his duty to—"

"You're kidding, right?"

I walked over to the condiment bar and filled a bigger ramekin. An agent materialized beside me as if I'd rubbed a lamp. "Miss. Please allow me."

"This isn't for him. It's for me."

"Please."

I surrendered the ketchup and rolled my eyes in Lissa's direction while she tried to keep a straight face and failed.

Great. And here I was, narrowly avoiding a tug-of-war over who was going to present His Highness with a dish of ketchup. I suddenly felt as if we were six again, fighting over who was going to get the last fig in the dish or who would ride in the front of the car to the village to get ice cream.

The fact that I could remember that distant holiday at all amazed me. I hadn't thought about it in years.

What I wanted was to be sitting next to a certain someone

the way Gillian and Carly were, leaning on him if I wanted, maybe even feeling his arm slip around me. I'd share Danyel's dish any day.

Instead, I got another ramekin off the stack and filled it. With ranch dressing.

"Will you not share with me?" the prince asked when I came back with it.

"No. I changed my mind."

He looked completely crushed. "But I got this for you."

I put the dish down next to my plate and sat. "Dude. One, your bodyguard got it, and two, if I share it with you, you'll just hog it all again and leave me none. Now get over it and let me eat my lunch."

And wouldn't you know it, just as I said those last words, everyone in the vicinity decided to stop talking. My voice, cranky as the attention-seeking little kid I'd once been, practically echoed.

I wanted to drop through the floor.

At the table by the window, Vanessa Talbot got up and strolled over to us. "Your Highness, my friends and I would be honored if you'd share your lunch with us." She glanced at me out of the corner of her mascaraed eye and scooped up his plate and the ramekin of ketchup as though she'd been waiting tables half her life. "I love fish and chips, don't you? Come on with me."

His spine stiff with the offense I'd dished him, Rashid got up and followed her and his lunch to the other table, where Callum, DeLayne, Dani, and Emily made a big production out of making him comfortable and hanging on his every royal word.

Fine. Marvy. Exactly what I'd wanted in the first place.

I eyed the fries cooling on my plate.

And pushed them away.

✉

To: SHanna@spenceracad.edu
From: Dijon@gmail2.com
Date: September 28, 2009
Re: Hi

Lissa gave me your e-mail so I hope you don't mind me invading your inbox. Funny to think that just a week ago we were hanging out on the beach. Hope school's going OK. Also that you don't mind me joining your prayer circle by video. I felt like we were all connected and I wanted some way to keep feeling that. I'll give Lissa the YouSendIt link for the next one.

So . . . I'm curious. You hang with believers and go to church and prayer circle, but from what I can tell, you're not a believer yet? *Yet* is a pretty hopeful word though :)

I haven't forgotten what you said on the beach. You know, when I was leaving. I was so surprised that I didn't have an answer, even though you deserved one. It takes me a while to think things through. Drives Kaz nuts sometimes.

So, bottom line, I've been thinking about you. Maybe we can get to know each other this way, or I can call you. However you want to play it, I know one thing. I'll be praying for you.

Your friend (I hope),
Danyel

chapter 6

'D BEEN MEAN to the prince. We'd been friends once. We weren't now. So throw me in the dungeon.

I was still in a mood on Wednesday as I left core class (U.S. History, which is the catch-all where they put me because I'd designed my own curriculum) and headed to second-period math. Maybe my blues had as much to do with him as with spending the previous evening reading Danyel's e-mail and watching his new prayer video over and over again with the sound turned down so Carly and Mac wouldn't hear, and then seeing Rashid crossing the quad this morning after breakfast with DeLayne Geary, who just happened to be going to the library at the same time.

Like she ever went to the library for anything but the latest issue of *Vogue*.

What was I going to have to do to get Danyel's attention and make him think of me as more than just "your friend, Danyel"? Date a prince?

Oh, ha-ha. That Shani, what a joker.

And then, what do you know, Rashid himself walked into

the math classroom and took the seat across the aisle from me. One of his bodyguards took up his stance outside the door, feet planted and hands clasped loosely in front. The other stood against the rear wall of the classroom. I'm sure this was totally creeping out the faculty, but Mr. Jackson, the math teacher, ignored both of them and got down to business.

When he assigned us some statistics problems to work on after the lecture, I made the mistake of glancing to my left. Rashid smiled, as if he'd been sitting there watching me and waiting for me to look.

"I apologize if I offended you," he whispered. "As we were eating together yesterday."

"We were not *together*." I glanced toward the front, but Mr. Jackson was busy helping someone. "And you didn't offend me. I—I'm sorry I snapped at you."

"I accept your apology." He sounded so pleased, I almost wished I hadn't. "Please do me the honor of joining me today."

"I, um—" What was the protocol for turning down royalty, anyway? How come they didn't teach us *that* in etiquette? "I usually just eat with my friends. You're welcome to join us, if you want."

"Miss Hanna, is there something you want to share with the class?" Mr. Jackson materialized in front of me, his school tie lying limply down his shirt, as if it had given up all hope of style years ago.

"No, sir," I said.

"Then kindly stop the chatter and get on with your work."

"Mr. Jackson, it was my fault," Rashid said. "I asked her a question and she was obliged to answer."

Jackson looked flummoxed. Because everyone knows that if a prince talks to you, you *are* obliged to answer. You can't just ignore him. I mean, wars have broken out over that kind of thing.

"Right," he said after a moment. "Please remember that I do

the talking in my classroom, Your Highness. I'd appreciate it if you'd confine your remarks to solutions to these problems."

"Yes, sir," we both mumbled.

I glanced at Rashid, and his eyes practically danced with suppressed laughter. An answering smile quivered on my mouth before I controlled myself and looked down at my text-book. He didn't have to come to my rescue. And he didn't have to think Jackson's pompousness was funny.

What was funny was a guy like him having a sense of humor. How could you have perfect grammar and the ability to laugh at things at the same time? I didn't need another reason to like the guy. And I really didn't want to remember that sparkle in his eyes.

No. Uh-uh. My heart belonged to Danyel.

DGeary	Help me? I need some info.
CAragon	This is a surprise.
DGeary	Why surprise? All Brett's friends are friends. Cool?
CAragon	I hope it's not math-related. Calculus. Blech.
DGeary	Man-related.
CAragon	Sorry, wrong number.
DGeary	Ha. What's with Shani and the prince?
CAragon	??
DGeary	Emily sent me a text second period. She thinks something's going on.
CAragon	She's overthinking.
DGeary	Emily has a hard time getting to think, never mind overthink. No, huh?
CAragon	I have inside info. Definitely no.
DGeary	Good.
CAragon	Why?
DGeary	Thanks. Gotta go.

AT LUNCH, RASHID took me up on my offer and staked
out our tables. He'd even had the bodyguards—let's call them
the BGs for short, okay?—push them together. Within minutes, the rowing team showed up and mobbed it, then Carly
and Brett, and finally, my girls.

Somebody must have taken the prince aside and given him
the dish on high school social skills. Or maybe he was a quick
study. Anyway, there was no hogging of ketchup or sly remarks
about couples. Instead, the guy acted like a normal person—or
as normal as you can be when your net worth has nine zeros.

Carly leaned over under the cover of a series of good-
natured insults about international soccer teams. "There's
weirdness afoot."

"What else is new?"

"DeLayne Geary IM'd me to find out if you and Rashid had
a thing."

I don't know which was more surprising: DeLayne speaking voluntarily outside her caste, or her asking nosy questions
about me. I don't think we've said more than six words to each
other since we parted ways in freshman year.

"What'd you tell her?"

"I said I had the inside scoop. Definitely no." She gave me
the kind of look that sees into your brain. "I hope that was
right."

"Of course it was right. Are you kidding me?"

She leaned back. "Just checking."

I grabbed her arm before she got out of whisper space. "I'm
serious. There is no thing. You know how I feel about—about
someone else." I stopped as Tate leaned between us to set down
a plate piled high with enough triple chocolate cake to put us
all into orbit for the afternoon.

Not quite enough to go around, however, when half your table is jocks. A minute later, Lissa reached for the empty plate. Rashid stopped her. "Allow me."

He took it to the dessert bar and loaded it up again. But instead of giving it to Lissa so she could start it around to everyone who'd missed out, he held it out to me.

"Please."

"Uh. Thanks." This guy really was a quick study. Not to mention good at improv—he'd gone from being served by the BGs to serving random girls in twenty-four hours flat.

Lissa pounced on the next piece of cake, and within seconds the rest of it was gone. "Thanks, Rashid." He looked pleased, a little smile curving his mouth. I guess when it's the first time you've ever served someone, you'd want to know they appreciated it.

A glance at the clock told me I had just enough time to scoot upstairs and grab my philosophy books and the music I'd chosen for Individual Voice this afternoon. "See you later," I told Lissa. "What's going on after school? Anything interesting?"

"Nothing. Call me and we'll figure something out."

Philosophy is really math disguised as critical thinking and logic, and it's a lot harder than you'd think. But my other choices in that time slot were O-Chem and six different flavors of algebra, so I took what I could get.

Voice was a different thing. I know I'm not going to be the next Mahalia Jackson—and by the end of two lessons, my instructor did, too. But I didn't care. If Carly could take design modules just because she loves them, then I could take voice and chorus for the same reason. Besides, a person deserves a little fun when she's a senior. We've earned it.

I let myself into our room, feeling pretty happy about the work I'd done on my scales and a first run-through of the gospel piece I'd chosen. I found Carly already there, changing out of her uniform.

"Hey." I couldn't wait to get out of mine, too. Say what you will about the hypo-allergenic fabric our plaid pleated skirts are made of, they're still . . . plaid pleated skirts.

"There you are." She laced up her sneakers. "I wanted to talk to you before Mac gets back."

I was slowly getting used to our room's new look. I'd pushed my bed back against the wall, and Mac and Carly had formed an L-shape with theirs. Mac didn't have a desk, but since she never used one anyway, it didn't matter. I hadn't found her in here doing homework once. Maybe she went to the library. Maybe she didn't do it. None of my nevermind.

"What's up?" I pulled on a glittery butterfly T-shirt—it had no slogans, so technically I could wear it outside class—and my comfiest black Theory jeans. "Lissa said she'd be up for something later. I vote for retail therapy."

"I wasn't thinking about tonight. What are you doing Friday night?"

That was easy. "Big bunches of nothing. Why?"

"Oh, good." She sat cross-legged on her bed, facing me. "What do you think about going out with me and Brett?"

"Uh." How to put this nicely? "You guys need a chaperone or what? Because that's *so* not the image I want going around."

"No, no." She laughed. "Are you kidding? I meant as a double. The four of us."

"The fourth being . . . ?" Hope sparked inside. Was Danyel coming up for the weekend? Why hadn't Lissa said anything?

"The prince, silly. Unless you have some other local guy you haven't told me about?"

I stared at her, my brain all wound up on the thought of Danyel while it tried to process the unexpected reality of Rashid. "What?"

"You and the prince. Me and Brett. On a double," she said

slowly, as though she were reading a primer to a first grader. "We were thinking dinner at TouTou's."

My brain and my mouth finally synced up. "If you think I'm asking the prince out to dinner, you've got another think coming."

"You don't have to ask him. He already asked us. And now I'm asking you."

"Wait a minute. I'm his date and I'm the last to know?" I didn't know whether to be insulted or not. "How come you get to be the messenger?"

"Farrouk explained it all to me."

"And Farrouk would be . . ."

"His Secret Service guy. The one who sleeps across his threshold at night."

"He does not."

"Yeah, he does. He's got one of those army cots and they move it every morning. The other guy's name is Bashir. He sleeps next door. They switch off every week."

I so didn't need to know this. "How do you know so much about the royal sleeping arrangements?"

"Because I asked them. They're really nice guys. And I had to talk to somebody while the prince was asking Brett if we could double. Then Brett asked me—I said yes, what a no-brainer—and I'm to ask you."

I had to sit down. "Carly, in case no one explained this to you yet, the guy is supposed to ask the girl. Not ask the girl's boyfriend to ask the girl's roommate to ask her."

"Not when you're a prince, apparently. See, he can't be turned down."

"Oh, no?"

"No, literally. He can't. It's some protocol thing. So by me asking you, he saves face." She gave me a big, sunny smile. "So what do you say?"

"I say this is insane. I thought you were going to tell me Danyel was in town." My shoulders slumped. "I think I'd give anything if he'd ask me out."

"Don't tell Rashid he's the consolation prize. But at the same time, having a prince for second choice isn't so bad. Look on the bright side. It could be Rory Stapleton."

In spite of myself, a laugh bubbled out of me. "I wouldn't go out with that guy if he was the last man standing after the apocalypse."

"So the prince isn't so bad?"

"No, he isn't." I flipped open the philosophy textbook next to me and closed it again. "The grown-up version is kind of growing on me. In fact, if the memory of him stealing my figs didn't get in the way, I'd think he was pretty hot."

"Go buy yourself some figs and get over it. Please say you'll come. You can still like Danyel, who, may I remind you, hasn't exactly been pounding down your door. There's nothing wrong with going out with friends—and Rashid qualifies as an old friend. I think it would be fun."

"We don't have to worry about them being able to pick up the tab, that's for sure."

She snorted. "Don't say you like the food. The prince might buy the place and give it to you."

"Oh, no." I wagged a finger at her. "He can't do that. Brett's family already owns it."

"They do not. I found that out awhile ago."

"I can't believe it. I thought you only ate at places they own."

"Do they own Starbucks? Huh?" She threw an embroidered pillow at me.

"Not yet. Give them time." I lobbed it back.

"So you'll go? I can tell him yes?"

"Yes, yes already, I'll go. I can't turn down my best friend."

Even if she was a stand-in for a guy who was too hot for his own good.

And mine.

⊚

Dijon	You forgot to give me your cell number in your e-mail last night.
SHanna	Oops. 847-555-2112.
Dijon	Tx. Glad you liked the video.
SHanna	I still think it feels weird to be prayed for.
Dijon	I'll stop if you want :)
SHanna	I said weird. Not bad :)
Dijon	If you ever get the urge, pray for Lissa's folks.
SHanna	Her, too. Does she talk to you?
Dijon	Some stuff. Mostly she talks to Kaz.
SHanna	Bet that makes him happy.
Dijon	Oh, yeah.
SHanna	How can she not know he's in love with her?
Dijon	He wrote *Blue Day* for her and told me he'd refinish my fav board if I'd sing it.
SHanna	That was for HER?
Dijon	::nods::
Dijon	Shani?
Dijon	OK 'bye.

chapter 7

HOW MANY GIRLS does it take to get ready for dinner with a prince?

Five.

And you thought I was telling a joke, didn't you? Let me tell you now—this was no joke.

"Expect the paparazzi," Mac told Carly and me, her tone as serious as that of a commander sending troops into battle. "Dress as though you're going to be posted on WhoWhatWear Daily-dot-com, because you are."

"I am *so* glad you're here," I said with complete sincerity. "I totally did not want to hear that, but you're right."

"Of course." She made herself more comfortable on her bed. Of the five of us, she was the most qualified to be going out with Rashid, what with the title and all. I had no idea what I was doing. If it had been left up to me, I'd have probably pulled on my skinny jeans and a slinky top and done something fun with my hair. But no way did I want to be the Mistake of the Day on the fashion sites. And it wasn't because of Rashid.

Odds were Danyel would see any pictures, because of course

Lissa would oh-so-innocently send them to him and Kaz. Friends shared things, didn't they? And if we were all going to be just friends, then a picture of me looking fabulous on a prince's arm was no skin off anyone's nose, was it?

Ha. Lissa is so devious. And she's on my side. Something else to be glad about.

"Too bad everyone's already seen the Herrera. It would have been perfect." Lissa and Mac were going through my closet, item by item. Lissa held up a ruffled yellow Biba silk with cut-out shoulders. "What about this?"

"Too fussy." Mac shook her head. "She needs a statement dress that will photograph well no matter how it's lit. That one will go transparent. We'll take some shots with my digital when we decide, just to make sure."

I never thought about being lit. Or making a statement, or taking pictures while I got dressed. I just bought things because I liked them.

"Wait—what's that?" Mac dove and came up holding a spill of lime-green jersey. "Is this a Cavalli?" I nodded. "Put it on."

I'd bought it because I liked the Greek vibe—you know, like a Doric chiton. Now I was glad at least something in my closet had netted Mac's approval. I slithered into it and glanced at my girls. "Uh, just a sec." I had a pair of gold Prada high-heeled sandals here . . . where were they? Aha! I stepped into them and then presented my changed-up self for inspection.

Four pairs of eyes gave me the once-over.

"Gold hoops," Carly said thoughtfully. "Big ones."

"And I have a gold necklace I can lend you," Lissa said.

We all looked at Mac. She narrowed her eyes and fetched the camera. "Pose."

I vamped in three different directions while she snapped pictures. Then she plugged the camera into her laptop, brought the shots up and considered them, nibbling the inside of her

lip. We crowded in behind her, looking at the pictures and waiting. Then she nodded, once. "You'll do. The Greek look is a
nice nod to your past together. Go dramatic on the makeup.
And the hair."

If there was one thing I could do without help, it was that.
By the time I had my face on, they'd pooled their resources,
and Carly turned slowly in the middle of the room in a drop-
dead Sonia Rykiel leather skirt with a discreetly ruffled Miu
Miu blouse so fine, you could pull it through the proverbial
wedding ring. (And the camera test proved that her cami, at
least, wasn't transparent.) Gillian lent her a pair of diamond
earrings that had to be a couple of carats each, and once I'd
finished pulling my hair into a quasi-Greek knot, I did hers.

"You have great hair," I told Carly, pulling it to the crown of
her head and rolling the fall of curls around my fingers. "You're
so lucky."

"I'm lucky to have friends like you guys," she said quietly.
"This is the best part."

"What, are you saying our night can only go downhill from
here?" I was only half joking. At least she had Brett to fall back
on. If my half of the date turned out to be a disaster, all I could
do was find the nearest cab and head for the hills.

"You know what I'm saying. All of us helping each other.
That's the part I like."

And then it was time.

Brett called the room phone from the reception hall and we
scrambled to finish our hair, then locate bags and wraps. Only
fifteen minutes later, while Gillian, Lissa, and Mac ranged
along the upper balustrade to watch, we descended the marble
staircase like debs being presented at the ball.

I remember Brett sucking in a breath as he looked at Carly.
And the scent of the freesia in a big bowl at the bottom of
the steps.

But mostly I remember Rashid in a flawlessly cut Savile Row suit and tie, gazing up at me with those dark brown eyes as though I were some Olympian goddess, about to give him a golden apple.

"You look ravishing." He picked up my hand and kissed it, and goose bumps tiptoed all the way up my arm to my neck and up the back of my skull.

Whoa. *And that was just your hand.*

I couldn't think things like that. I'd blush and go all weird, and he'd wonder what was wrong with me. I had to play it cool. Princes were still guys. I'd treat him like . . . like the friends we could have been, if we hadn't lived on opposite sides of the planet.

Except the way he looked at me didn't feel like "just friends."

The limo waiting in the sweep of the driveway was so big, I hardly registered the presence of the BGs—Farrouk and Bashir, I mean, though I couldn't tell who was who. Brett opened a couple of sparkling waters, poured them into glasses, and squeezed fresh lime into them from a dish of ice waiting at his elbow. I could have ridden around all night like this, but it takes longer to park a limo this size than it does to drive to TouTou's.

The driver got out to open the door and I caught Carly's eye.

Statement, she mouthed silently, and grinned.

Because Mac was right.

I don't know how they'd got wind of it, but a cloud of paparazzi coalesced out of nowhere. I took a deep breath, put my shoulders back, and slid out of the limo Pradas first, pushing off with my leg muscles instead of getting out head and torso first. That, you'll remember, is how the paparazzi got that big old cleavage shot of Lady Diana at the Goldsmiths' Hall back in 1981. My cleavage is my business.

When the prince came out after me and offered me his arm, the evening lit up like a lightning strike with all the flashes going off. Somehow Brett and Carly positioned themselves in front of us in a protective barrier, and the four of us walked as quickly as the crowd would let us into the vestibule of the restaurant.

The doorman closed the door behind us and the BGs took up a fighting stance just inside, in case anyone decided to rush the door for a final shot.

"Wow," Carly breathed as she let her wrap slide down her shoulders. The diamonds in her ears caught some serious sparkle from the lighting overhead. "That's gotta be a first for me."

"Consider it practice for the movie premiere," I murmured.

Brett stepped up to the glass table where the hostess smiled, waiting. "Loyola, party of four."

She glanced at the leather book. Just a formality, I was sure. Because of course the whole restaurant had already been re-conned by the BGs, and everyone had probably brushed up on their royal protocol once they knew the prince was coming.

The hostess looked up. "I'm sorry, I'm afraid there's no table for you."

"There is," Brett said. "I booked it myself a couple of days ago."

"Sir, we book at least a month in advance."

"I was assured we had a reservation. I'm Brett Loyola, from Spencer." He lowered his voice. "And Prince Rashid of Yasir is in our party. Even if there is some kind of mistake, I'm sure you know about that."

She looked over at Rashid and me, and her face paled. "One moment, sir." She vanished into the back, behind a huge vase filled with flowers.

"Is everything all right?" one of the BGs asked Brett. "I did the security check myself, yesterday. You were to have the corner table, between the two windows."

I leaned over to look into the dining room. "That table's empty. And there's even a waiter standing next to it. They seem to be ready for us."

Brett moved as if to go in, when a man in a suit came around the vase, the hostess right behind him. "Mr. Loyola?"

With a smile, Brett said, "It's okay. I see our table. We'll just go in now."

"Mr. Loyola, wait, please."

Both Brett and the prince raised an eyebrow. It would have been funny if I hadn't felt so uncomfortable. There was something in the man's tone I didn't like.

"My name is Antonio Edgardo. I'm the manager of TouTou's. I'm afraid I have some . . . unfortunate news."

"Did something happen?" I couldn't help it. I had to ask.

He glanced at me, then at the prince. "No, miss. But I am afraid we'll be unable to serve you today."

All of us stared. The dining room was only three-quarters full, and our table was ready and waiting. Brett found his voice first. "What do you mean? Our table's right there."

"That is reserved for another party."

"But the prince's security said it was for us."

The manager nodded toward the BGs, who were both frowning. "I'm sorry. The gentleman is mistaken. We are unable to serve you today."

"Yeah, I heard you the first time," Brett said. "What I want to know is, why?"

"I'm not at liberty to say."

"Who's the other party?" Carly asked suddenly. "At that table, I mean."

The manager looked relieved, as if here was a question he had an answer to. "That table is reserved for the Talbot party, miss."

"Talbot," I repeated. "As in, Vanessa?"

"Yes, miss. Now, may I ask you to leave?"

"You may not." The BGs' frowns were nothing to the one Rashid was sporting. "My party cannot be turned away. It is impossible."

"I apologize, Your Highness." The manager actually half bowed. "I deeply regret our inability to serve you. I hope you will enjoy yourselves very much at another establishment."

"I don't believe this," Brett breathed.

I gripped the prince's arm and tugged. "Come on. We're out of here. I'm not going to give Vanessa Talbot the satisfaction of seeing pictures of us getting kicked out. Who's for Lori's Diner?"

"Me!" Carly said with a bright smile. "I'd kill for one of her burgers."

Rashid looked as though he was about to declare World War III. "I am not leaving. I wish to speak to the owner."

I looked him in the eye. "We've been set up, Rashid. Vanessa did this to embarrass us. To embarrass you. She probably called the tabs and told them to be here, too."

Carly stepped closer, eyes snapping. "We're going to act as if we just came for a soda, and we're going to climb into that limo looking like we're having the time of our lives. Total jealousy-making pictures will result. She's not going to win this one." She glanced at the manager, and the snap in her eyes turned to withering scorn. "Everyone knows they serve alcohol to minors here because of her, anyway."

Before Brett and Rashid could say another word, the BGs flung the doors open. I pulled Rashid out beside me and pasted on an "I'm living the high life and don't you hate me for it?" smile. We trooped out onto the sidewalk, laughing and talking while the flashes popped and somebody gabbled descriptions of our dresses into a handheld recorder.

When the doors shut behind us and the limo pulled out into

traffic, I drew a deep breath and sank back onto the leather cushions. "And the Oscar goes to . . ."

"I have never been so humiliated in my life." Rashid's tone held deadly calm. The kind that comes before the storm. "If it had not been for you, I would have ordered the owner to explain himself to me—and then serve me himself. On his knees."

"It's not their fault, Rashid. Vanessa obviously has some serious clout there. This might be your only visit, but she's there constantly. They'd probably go out of business without her."

Rashid turned to Carly. "What was that you said back there? About alcohol?"

She shrugged and glanced at Brett, then back at Rashid. "They serve alcohol to minors. I've been there when they've done it. That's why Vanessa always has her meetings and things in the upstairs room. So no one sees."

His eyes narrowed. "So this is illegal, then?"

"Very much so."

"Ah." He sat back and didn't say another word until we arrived at the diner.

We may have been insanely overdressed for it, but in San Francisco, a woman—or a man—can go to McDonald's in sequins and a feather boa and no one looks twice. The BGs requested a separate table and settled in with glasses of iced tea a few seats away. We ordered up our burgers and when they came, I felt relieved when Rashid made no moves at all on my ketchup.

In fact, he behaved like a normal guy—if normal means perfect manners and interesting conversation. Okay, so he's messing up the bell curve. I still appreciated it, even if all we were talking about was school.

"So what concentration are you working on?" he asked me. "If Carly's is history and Brett's is math?"

I lifted a shoulder in a half shrug. "Technically, it's an

individual concentration, but what that works out to is economics. They've let me build my own out of math, political science, and history."

"In order to do what?" Carly asked. "Sounds brutal."

I nodded. "It is, but it's interesting. My dad runs this massive petroleum company. I haven't really talked it over with him, but I figure once I bag my M.B.A. at Northwestern or Harvard Business School or Stanford, I can go to work for him."

"You're really looking out there into the future." Brett bit into his kosher pickle. "I figure I'm doing good knowing when midterms are."

"Yeah, I worry about those, too. What about you, Rashid? What do you want to do?" The second the words were out, I wanted to kick myself. What else was he going to do but run a country?

He smiled at me in a way that made me feel as if my question wasn't so stupid. "A ruler must know many things. Politics, economics, languages. I am here for two reasons. One is to take a term of computer science, with tutoring every week from experts in Silicon Valley. I plan on a doctorate from Oxford in political science, even though my father would rather I went into the military."

"I'd stick with Oxford," Brett said.

"We are in agreement."

"What's the second reason?" I asked.

Rashid smiled at me. "To see my childhood friend again, of course. I am glad to see we share an interest in politics and economics. I do not doubt you will be running your father's company when I am running my father's kingdom."

I had to laugh at the thought. "Maybe when we're fifty. But first things first. College apps and scores and all that red tape."

"Let's not talk about that," Carly said. "It's Friday night, we're out on the town with two hot men, and we can sleep in tomorrow. It doesn't get better than that."

"Yes, it does." Brett patted the chest pocket of his jacket. "I happen to have four tickets to Luna's, if anybody feels like going."

"Who's playing?" I demanded, hardly able to believe it. Luna's brought in the coolest acts for intimate performances. People lined up for blocks, but you either had to be on a list or have a look the bouncers liked. And sometimes even that didn't work. Then another thought hit me. "Not that it matters. You have to be twenty-one to get in."

"Not on nights they don't serve alcohol. Which would be tonight, because it's a family show."

"Whose family?" Carly asked.

"Oh, just the Dylans." Brett grinned as album covers flipped in our heads.

"Dylans," I said. "As in Bob and Jakob?"

"Yep."

Carly and I shrieked and leaped up to hug him. I knew for a fact that show had sold out to subscribers before the box office even opened. I'd never seen Bob Dylan live before, and how cool was it that being in the prince's party made sure we had seats on the edge of the stage?

The evening was like something out of someone else's life. I mean, I've had some pretty good seats at concerts before. Season tickets on the court at Bulls games. But I've never been escorted to my table by the club manager himself, or been taken backstage to meet a legend and his son at a whispered request.

When we finally fell into the limo at one in the morning, chattering a mile a minute while the final encore still played in my head, I had to conclude that dating a prince definitely had its perks.

The limo pulled up at Spencer's front steps. As I got out, I felt like Cinderella coming home after the ball, or, to use one of Lissa's sci-fi references, Luke coming back to boring old Tatooine after saving the galaxy.

The prince and the BGs climbed out after me. After a second, I realized Carly and Brett weren't following, and a second after that, I realized why.

My face heating in a blush, I practically ran through the doors.

The BGs marched up the staircase, presumably to flush bad guys out of Rashid's dorm room, which left the two of us standing in the reception hall. The normal weekday curfew of lights-out at ten p.m. was suspended on weekends. The only light came from a couple of the wall sconces and the upstairs hallway. The stairs were a swath of shadow.

I paused on the bottom step. "Well. Um. Thank you for a wonderful evening. I've never had one like it. Even being kicked out of TouTou's turned out to be fun."

"I am glad you had a good time." He leaned on the banister, one shallow marble step below me. This put our eyes on the same level. "I, too, have never had one like it."

"Really?" I whispered. He stood close. Closer. "Rashid?"

His eyes held pools of darkness. "I love the sound of my name on your lips."

Oh, my. What a romantic thing to say. But I had no business getting romantic with him.

You want to.

I shouldn't. I told Danyel I liked him.

Danyel isn't here.

"Rashid, did you mean what you said before? That you came to Spencer partly because of me?"

"Yes. Our families have been connected since the sixteenth century."

I blinked. Is that what Mom had meant by "a bunch of history"? The mistress of the understatement, my mom.

"And you and I played together as children." He paused. "Of all the schools in this country, I wanted one where I knew a friend. School can be a very lonely place for someone in my position."

My heart melted. I'd had my own issues with people trying to cozy up so they could get things out of me. I could just imagine how it was for him, never knowing if he was liked for himself or for his money.

"I'm glad we are friends." Rashid leaned in, holding my gaze. My heart stopped melting and began to pound. I think I forgot to breathe. "And possibly—"

The front door swung open and Carly's voice called, "Good night" as the limo's engine started up outside and gravel crunched under its tires.

Rashid jerked back, and I found my guilty self halfway up the stairs before the door had even swung shut.

"Oh, hi, Rashid, are you still here?" Carly's light tones echoed in the midnight silence. "Where's Shani?"

But I didn't wait. The sound of my high heels clacking on the marble was too loud for me to hear his answer, anyway.

chapter 8

I ROLLED OUT OF BED just in time for brunch on Saturday, but only because Mac was making so much noise trying to be quiet that I finally gave up on sleep. Carly and I took turns in the shower and stumbled downstairs, where we gulped coffee and considered the waffle maker.

"Too much work," I finally muttered, and settled for fruit and yogurt.

Carly, for whom kitchen appliances will do backflips and spins, had a couple of waffles made in less time than it takes to tell about it, complete with raspberry syrup.

"About time you guys turned up." Gillian put her MacBook Air on the table and sat across from us. "We were going to send in the EMTs."

"It's Saturday. We'll sleep in if we want to," Carly informed her around a mouthful of waffle.

"I heard what happened."

"We got to see the Dylan show at Luna's," I told her. "It was amazing. Front row seats, and backstage passes. I met Bob Dylan. How cool is that?"

"*Très* cool," Gillian agreed. "But I meant before that. I heard about the fracas at TouTou's."

"TouTou's." Carly made the name sound like a snort. "I'm so over that place. What did you hear?"

Instead of answering, Gillian flipped open her notebook. SeenOn.com's lead article filled the screen.

Playboy Prince Does More Than Study

Look out, California fashionistas! Prince Rashid al Amir, who's spending an exchange term at the elite Spencer Academy boarding school in San Francisco, is already hitting more than the books.

Spotted last night arriving at TouTou's, celebrity hangout and *de rigeur* stop for a night on the town, were the prince, the Loyola dynasty heir, and two love-lies who may have been unknown to this writer, but who definitely have their style chops down. Check the Roberto Cavalli and the more conservative choice of the just-out Rykiel leather mini. Spencer students? Or budding style icons? Only their publicist knows for sure—until we find out more.

"Doesn't sound like a fracas to me. Check out these pictures." I studied a profile shot of Carly and me. "Lucky I remembered to suck in my stomach when I got out of the car. That dress has zero forgiveness."

"You have zero stomach," Gillian reminded me. "I bet your percentage of body fat is in the single digits."

"Nope. But my mom's right, on the rare occasions she dishes maternal advice. Good posture hides a multitude of sins."

"Funny you should mention sins," Gillian said in a smooth

segue, "because I hear there was more to this story than your Prada sandals."

"Such as?" Carly prompted, with a glance at me.

Gillian leaned in. "Did you guys really get kicked out of TouTou's? Is that even possible?"

She looked so aghast that I couldn't help it. I laughed. "We were trying to keep it on the down low, but I guess that's too much to expect. Getting kicked out is only the beginning. And if you want accurate, we were *refused service*." I made quote marks in the air. "But you don't refuse service to the heir to the Lion Throne and get away with it. I predict the real fracas is yet to come."

"He was pretty ticked," Carly agreed. "He was going to make the owner serve him on his knees."

"I'd have bought a ticket to see that." Gillian leaned on both elbows, enthralled. "They seriously refused to serve you? No wonder SFTonight-dot-com said something nasty about you guys knocking back the fastest drinks in the west. Next thing you know, you'll all be alcoholics on the way to visit Betty Ford."

"That'll impress Rashid," Carly said. "He doesn't drink anything but water and iced tea."

I glanced around the nearly empty room. I didn't feel like dwelling on what I couldn't change. "Where's Lissa? And Jeremy?"

"Lissa went to get her hair trimmed," Gillian said. "Who's up for a group pedi and a hot stone massage this afternoon at the Tea House? She said she'd meet us there—we just need to call her."

Carly and I both put our hands up. "We'll tell Mac," Carly said. "*Chicas* only. It'll be fun."

"Lissa could use some fun," Gillian said. "While you guys were out last night, her dad came by and took her out for coffee."

Now that principal photography for *The Middle Window* was done, Gabe Mansfield holed up mostly on the Ranch doing post-production, or at the house in Santa Barbara, and only came into the city when he absolutely had to.

"That doesn't sound so bad," Carly said. "I'd love it if my dad did that."

"He had some news for her."

"Uh-oh." Not good.

Gillian nodded. "She needs some bestie-love right now. Her dad came to tell her that he and her mom decided to separate. Officially. With paperwork and everything."

"Oh, no." I sat back, my breakfast lying heavy in my stomach.

"That's the last stop before the D-word," Carly said in the voice of one who knows. "Poor Lissa."

"Her dad's pretty cut up about it, but he doesn't know what else to do. But with him working up here and Patricia still keeping not just her maiden name, but her house in Beverly Hills, you kinda have to wonder how long this has been in the works." Gillian closed her notebook and sighed. "Anyway, after they got back we had a long talk, and I tried to encourage her. It's not like it's her fault."

"Or that she can do anything to get them back together," Carly said.

"I officially declare this a man-free day," I said. "We're going to focus on Lissa today and nothing else."

"Build her and ourselves up," Gillian agreed, nodding. "Good plan."

"Done." Carly mopped up the last of her syrup. "Gillian, you call her and tell her we'll meet her at the Tea House at two. That'll give us all time to get it together and take a cab down there."

So, that afternoon found us kicked back in our chairs at

the Tea House, which really did serve green tea while the aestheticians massaged your legs with warm oil and hot, round stones before they got down to serious business with your feet.

"Bliss." Mac sighed as she chose a crisp ginger cookie off the tray. "This was a wonderful idea."

"I know why we're here," Lissa said. "You guys are the best friends ever."

Carly reached over and squeezed her hand on the padded arm of the chair. "We're so sorry about your parents. It totally wrecks."

Normally, Lissa looks as though she's walking around in her own personal sunbeam. It'd be enough to make you hate her, if you didn't like her so much. But now the beam was dimmed and her skin looked pale, even in the Tea House's flattering studio lights.

"You got that right. But, like Gillian told me yesterday, it's their thing. I still love them and I know they love Jolie and me." Her lower lip trembled, then firmed up. "But I still wish I could do something. Do you think if I moved home it would do any good?"

Lissa leave? Split up our gang? Bad enough it would happen when we graduated. No way could it be sooner than that. "But they aren't home," I said. "Your mom's not staying in Santa Barbara, is she?"

Lissa shook her head. "She's working on a big fund-raiser for Habitat for Humanity with Brad Pitt. That means she stays at her place in Beverly Hills."

"Is she going to the premiere with your dad?" Gillian wanted to know. "Because if it isn't all over the tabs now, it will be then."

"I don't think so," Lissa said. "He said something about that when he was here. I think I'm his date."

"Kaz won't like that," I said, my mouth five seconds ahead of my brain as usual.

"He's still coming." Obviously it had gone right past her. "You all are. The Saturday before Thanksgiving weekend. Don't forget—we're all going to L.A. and staying at Mom's."

"I can't wait," Carly said. "But won't that be awkward if we're at your mom's and we're going with your dad?"

Lissa shook her head. "That's the confusing part. They're not fighting or anything, and while we were having lunch, Dad called Mom to make sure she hadn't booked a limo for us, because he had one. Is that abnormal or what?"

"They're being civil because of you and your sister," Mac put in. "Putting a good face on it. Consider yourself lucky they aren't throwing vases and shrieking."

"So that's the thing—where would you move?" I asked. "Even if you went to live in L.A., what good would that do?"

"I know, I know." Lissa's hands flopped uselessly on the arms of the chair. "But I can't help thinking that my being around one of them at least might help. That I could talk to Mom and maybe change her mind."

"You're talking to her now," Gillian pointed out. "So is your dad and probably your sister, too. Lots of talk and it makes no difference."

"It'd be different in person."

"I don't know," Carly said. "I was right in the same house with both my parents and nothing I said did any good. They still split."

"Is your mother still going to marry that man you don't like?" Mac asked, her eyes closed. Her chair hummed as it gave her a back massage.

Carly made a face and nodded. "Nothing I say does any good there, either. She's acting like everything's peachy and Richard Vigil is one of my best buds. I got an e-mail this morning telling me to go to some wedding site that tells you the best bridesmaid dress for your figure type. Like I didn't know that already."

"I think a butt bow would be perfect for your figure type," Mac said, deadpan.

"And ruffles." Gillian sat up as the aesthetician wrapped her calves in a steaming white towel. "Lots and lots of ruffles. Below the knee. Ooh, a fishtail gown with ruffles. And a butt bow. Can you see it?"

"The horror! The horror!" Lissa covered her eyes, flinching away from Carly, who was sitting on her right.

"You guys, that would be totally wrong for her," I told them. "You know she secretly wants the Scarlett O'Hara dress, complete with floppy hat and parasol."

Lissa pretended to gasp and pressed both hands to her chest. "Oh, Mama," she said in her best Georgia accent, "a butt bow just for me. You shouldn't have, bless your heart."

"Stop, stop!" Carly waved her hands. "My eyes are bleeding—don't make me look in the mirror!"

Behind her hands, Carly flashed a look at me. That girl would make fun of her own self all afternoon if it would bring the light back into Lissa's face. And by four o'clock, when we left all buffed and polished and (in my case) sporting Chocolate Shakespeare on my toes, we'd done some good work in cheering her up and helping her remember there were still reasons to smile left in the world.

After all: Carly in a butt bow. How good can it get?

When I turned my phone on in the cab on the way back (there being a silly no-cell-phone rule in the spa), I already had three messages. I goggled at the message screen. Two from Rashid and one from Danyel? *Whoa. Better stop at the 7-11 and buy a lottery ticket, too.* But I couldn't call either of them from in the cab, squashed as I was between Gillian and Mac. Instead, I had to wait until we got back to school and everyone clattered up the staircase to the dorm. I slipped out into the deserted quad and sat at a table in the sun.

Wow. Not one, but two guys trying to get to me. How cool was that? Though my first instinct was to call Danyel, Rashid had left two messages. If it was something important, I needed to call him back before I found Farrouk looming out of the shadows and hauling me away by the arm.

He answered his cell on the first ring. "Shani. I have missed you."

Missed me like his call rolled to voicemail or missed me like a guy missed a girl? Never mind. I had no business thinking like that. "I had to do an intervention for a friend." I left off the details. "What's up?"

"I had hoped to catch you earlier to see if we could study together."

"Oh, I'm sorry I missed it. Homework on a Saturday afternoon? That sounds like gobs of fun."

"Gobs? My English is very good but I have not heard of this before."

"Sorry. Lots of fun."

"With you, even the gross national product of Canada would be fun."

He sounded so sincere that I laughed. It was true that with the right company, homework could not only be fun, but romantic. It wasn't my fault I was thinking romance. I'd made it all the way through high school without anything you could remotely call a date, and now suddenly two guys were on the hook. What was that song? It's raining men?

"Would you like to go out this evening?" the prince asked. "I promise it will not be dinner at TouTou's."

I laughed. "Fine by me. Listen, what kind of music do you like?"

"I like what you like."

"Give me a break, Rashid. Tell the truth."

"I like hip-hop and flamenco and Tchaikovsky and the music from the streets and bazaars of my country."

"Have you ever heard the blues? Live?"

"No, never."

"I saw a poster downtown that Kenny Wayne Shepherd was playing at the Fillmore. He's great. You'd like him."

"I am sure I will. I will have Bashir arrange for tickets and dinner."

"I can do that, Rashid. Don't bother the guy when he's busy watching for ninjas in the bushes."

"It is his duty. Seven o'clock?"

"Meet you in the lobby."

"I look forward to it as I would the dawn."

I hung up before I started to babble. No one had ever told me *that* before. I wasn't even sure why I'd agreed to go out with him, except that I had silky legs and brand-new toes and both of them were ready to party.

Shaking my head at my bad self, I scrolled to Danyel's message and hit Send.

"Hey, Shani, thanks for calling me back." If Rashid's voice was like midnight and scratchy stars, Danyel's was smooth dark chocolate. A singer's voice. Yum.

"No problem. We were out giving Lissa some group therapy over a pedicure."

"Oh, man. Bless you for that. Is she okay?"

"She's pretty cut up. I would be, too. She's in problem-solving mode. She doesn't get that she's not the one who can solve the problem."

"I know. Kaz and Gillian have been tag-teaming her."

"At least between Carly and Mac we've got lots of experience in breakups of the parental kind. So they've been trying to help, too."

"She really lucked out with you guys. I have to say, I didn't want her to go to that school. I thought it would mess with her head. But meeting you and the others must've been a God thing."

I wasn't sure I wanted to have a supporting role in the Big Guy's plans, 'cuz then it wouldn't be too much of a stretch to have Him notice me for real. I was still learning about the effect He had on people—I wasn't sure I was ready for His effect on me.

"I'm glad they're my friends, too." I paused long enough so he'd know I was changing channels. "So, what's new with you?"

"Well . . . guess where I am right now?"

"Um, let's see. Probably sitting on the beach with your board stuck in the sand, looking out over the waves and wondering if there's time to get in one more before you call it a day."

"Try again."

"You and Kaz are four-wheeling somewhere and the beauty of nature made you think of me."

"Nope."

No looking forward to the dawn for this guy. "I give up."

"I'm at my sister's apartment in Daly City. Got any plans tonight?"

My mouth dropped open. Danyel was at this moment seven stops away on BART. He was in town for the weekend. He was asking me out.

And I'd just agreed to go to a concert with the prince.

I clutched my forehead with my free hand. Give the girl a love life and what does she do with it?

Gets it totally twisted.

chapter 9

WHY HADN'T I answered their messages in the opposite order? It wasn't like I could call Rashid back and say, "Oops, forgot I had to wash my hair." Stuff like that sparks international incidents where ambassadors have to be called in to mediate.

Danyel cleared his throat. "Shani? You there?"

"I'm here. Just having a moment, is all."

"Did you get my e-mail?"

"Uh-huh. I got all of them."

"So this isn't a total surprise."

"Your being in town sure is."

He chuckled. "I thought it might be. But the rest . . . I mean, after what you said to me on the beach, I figured I was pretty safe in asking."

"The thing is—I mean, I wish I didn't, but I already have plans."

He took a second to absorb this. "Oh. Well, yeah, I'm sure you do. It is kind of last minute. But I thought, um . . ."

The last thing I wanted was to embarrass him. "What about

tomorrow? I usually to go out to Marin with Lissa and my girls, but something tells me she's going to want to go to the Ranch and have her dad to herself. I bet she cuts us loose over breakfast."

"I'ma go to church with my sister and her family, and then I gotta hit the road back to S.B."

No way could he come all this way and not see me. That was just wrong. "I could meet you for breakfast, maybe."

"Why don't you come to Sol and Malika's? I'd like them to meet you. Then you could come to church with us." I hesitated, and he picked up on it right away. "Or not, if the church thing makes you uncomfortable."

"No, no, it's fine. I go to church with Lissa and them, no problem."

"So I'm still waiting for an answer on that."

"What?" But I already knew. I was just stalling for time, trying to figure out what to say.

"About whether you're a believer or not."

"How come it matters so much to you? I mean, I thought we had it goin' on when we were all at Lissa's."

"Yeah, we did, but for me there has to be more to it than that."

"Like what?"

"Can we have this conversation in person? Like, tomorrow? Because I think it's important and I want to be with you when we talk."

I homed in on *I want to be with you*. Now, that's what I was talking about. "Okay. What's the address? I'll catch a cab."

"No, you won't. I'll pick you up at eight."

"In the *morning*?" I was gonna be so wrecked, getting up that early after seeing Kenny Wayne Shepherd.

He hesitated for a second, then laughed. "Uh, yeah. Breakfast usually does involve morning. Malika says we leave for church at ten thirty."

"Okay, eight it is. See you then."

I disconnected and tucked my phone in my Bottega bag. Then I watched the sun slip behind the Spanish tiles of the roof of the classroom wing opposite.

Dates with two guys in twenty-four hours. Who'd have thought?

....

✉

To: shanna@spenceracad.edu
From: beryl.hanna@petronova.com
Date: October 3, 2009
Re: London calling

Hi Baby,

We're still here while Daddy does business. I went to the V&A myself just for fun to see the exhibit on royal wedding dresses. Haven't been there in years.

Speaking of royals, I caught a certain little article on a certain Web site featuring my own girl on the arm of a certain royal someone! I'm glad you're getting to know the prince. You better dish me the details because I sure don't want to find out from People.com.

Love, Mama
....

"I HEAR WE'RE sort of related."

In the fifteen-minute break between Kenny Wayne's sets,

we'd slipped out of the theater and snagged a Coke in a frosty glass for me and an iced tea for the prince. Well, Bashir had snagged them. All we had to do was appear at the door and have them presented to us. A girl could really get used to this. Not that it means anything. I'm just sayin'.

"I think not."

"True. My mom says my great-grandma married one of your uncles. What does that make us, fifth cousins twice removed?"

He smiled into my eyes. "It makes us a man and a woman who are simply having fun together. As I told you, our families have been connected for centuries." He glanced over his shoulder into the theater. "I like this Kenny Wayne Shepherd. He is very talented."

"And so are you. At avoiding the subject."

He took a sip of his drink. Around us, the lobby was full of people gabbing and laughing, dressed in everything from ripped jeans to silk. Me, I'd picked jeans too—my Citizens of Humanity black ones with my fierce red Dolce stilettos. Top that with a Max Azria chiffon blouse over a black lace tank and I was hot, in my oh-so-humble opinion.

And Rashid? He'd come to a blues concert in a double-breasted pinstriped suit with a collarless black silk shirt. I mean, not that I care or anything, but the man looked fine. We were collecting the looks like tickets at the door.

"I am not avoiding the subject. I would not be so rude. But I don't wish you to think of me as family. That would—how do I put it—spoil the fun."

"Believe me, sunshine, family isn't what I think of when I think of you."

"You think of me?"

I took a step back. "You're hard to avoid. And with Farrouk and Bashir, it's like there are three of you. If I don't see you, I see them, running around for you."

"It is their duty."

"So you keep saying. Don't they ever get a day off?"

"Yes. Alternate weekends, with a day during the week. But I do not wish to talk about them. I wish to talk about us."

I eyed him over the rim of my glass. "There's an 'us'?"

He smiled, and I swear knees melted all over the lobby. But not mine. Definitely not mine, nuh-uh.

"I would like to think so."

I stuck out a hip. "What are you getting at, Rashid?"

"I have been talking with Brett Loyola. We've become friends, I think."

I resisted the urge to make a joke about the *us* being him and Brett. I had a feeling he wouldn't take too kindly to a poke at his manliness, even from me. "Okay. What do you talk about?"

"Sports, classes. I am to try out for the rowing team. But also girls." He held up a finger. "Correction. One girl. You."

I had to laugh. "Rashid, don't talk *about* me, just talk *to* me. Cut out the middleman."

"Sometimes you are not the easiest to talk to. And I am—" He hesitated. "It is very important that I get the words right."

"What words?" As though someone had called time, people began to surge back into the theater. I pulled Rashid to the side. "Just spit them out, Rashid."

"The show will be starting in a moment."

"Never mind. I want to hear what you have to say."

He took a breath, as if to settle himself. "Very well. I wish—I want—that is, if you would like it, I—uh—"

Wow. It probably took a lot to rattle a prince so much he lost his words. What did he have to tell me that could be that important? All I wanted was a little conversation, you know? Not state secrets or anything.

He looked me in the eye and blurted, "I would like us to go out."

I blinked. "We are out. Do you want to leave?"

"No, no. Brett says this is how you say it. To hook up. To be boyfriend and girlfriend. Go out."

Behind the door, Kenny Wayne blasted into a cover of "Scuttlebuttin'" while I goggled at Rashid.

"Go out? Like, be a couple? You and me?"

"Yes." He smiled and rocked back on his heels, like he was happy I'd finally gotten it.

"Well, I, uh . . ." Oh, help. This wasn't what I'd planned at all. How was I supposed to get to know Danyel if I were the official consort of the prince? How would I sneak off to call Danyel with Farrouk and Bashir on hand at every moment, listening in?

And, most important, how was I going to explain to Rashid that I was having breakfast with someone else in—I glanced at my watch with its pretty little diamond where the twelve should be—nine hours and forty-five minutes?

"Um, Rashid, I really—this is so sudden."

That was the best I could do? Call up a line from a forties B-movie? Where was my gold-plated education when I needed it? *Etiquette module, hello? Need help, here.*

Behind him, Bashir held open the door. Blistering notes, almost too fast to hear, roared out into the lobby and I jumped. Farrouk took our glasses.

"It is a surprise, I know," Rashid said. He took my hand and tucked it into the crook of his elbow. So old school. His soft sleeve was hot from his body temperature. He was overheated. Stressed. As nervous about asking as I was about answering.

My shaky self-confidence staggered and stood up. "It is, but that's not a bad thing. Let's take it one day at a time, okay? I like you a lot, but I'm not into formal, especially with someone I used to make sandcastles with."

The smile was back. "As you say, one day at a time. Now, shall we hear the rest of the show?"

That wasn't going to be a problem. Kenny Wayne was in fine form, tearing up the air with his guitar. I sank into my chair and then into the music. In fact, I was so into it that it was a bit of a shock when Rashid reached over and covered my fingers with his.

And the funny thing? His hand felt really good.

If that doesn't mess you up, I don't know what will.

I have to say, even with his perfect grammar and custom-made suits, Rashid was fun to have around. When he got up with everyone else to dance in the aisle, Farrouk and Bashir stiffened and kept their thousand-yard stares scanning in every direction, but Rashid grabbed me right there in front of them.

So then I had to add *good dancer* to the list.

I mean, whether he was six or sixteen, this guy was hard not to like—and the fact that closed doors had a habit of swinging wide for him didn't hurt, either. Which was why we found ourselves at the afterparty with the band at Yoshi's, grooving to their headliner and trading banter at two in the morning.

I stopped looking at my watch after that. Once you get past midnight, it's all the same, anyway. All I know is, when we finally cruised up the school driveway, gravel crunching under the tires of the limo, there wasn't a light on anywhere in the building except for the dim sconces in the entry hall.

Wordlessly, Rashid took my hand and pulled me into the common room opposite the stairs, where it was so dark I could only see a little of his face as the light from the hall played over it.

I expected him to drop my hand and tell me something

romantic, like he couldn't wait for the dawn, but he didn't. Instead, he pulled me closer.

"Rashid?" I whispered uncertainly.

"I had so much fun tonight, Shani." His breath moved the little curls by my ear. "I wonder, will it always be like this?"

"It's only our first date," I said. "Last night didn't count. And I don't know." How many concerts and clubs did he plan to take me to? "I want you to tell me something. For real."

"Of course. I would never lie to you."

That's what guys always say, and you roll your eyes and hedge your bets. But for some reason, I believed Rashid. He was a stand-up guy who didn't, as Mac would say, mess you about. That's the only reason I had the guts to ask what I needed to know.

"Why me? Out of all the girls in this school, why pick me?"

He smiled. That much I could see from the hall lights. The dark hid his eyes and one side of his body. "You are modest, deep inside."

As opposed to my outside? What was wrong with red shoes and a flirty neckline? I pulled back a little. "What does that mean?"

"It is only one of many reasons. Our families. Our childhood memories. You have grown up to be beautiful and intelligent. You dress well and you have presence. But more than these, you are compassionate and loyal and fun. Does that satisfy you?"

"That little laundry list could apply to any one of my friends, too. Why not one of them?"

"Because I feel most comfortable with you. You do not treat me like a prince. You treat me like a friend. As though the years since our summers in Greece had not passed."

"But they did pass. I'm not that little girl anymore, Rashid."

"I know." He smiled in a way that told me he liked it that his friend was all grown up.

"And I have lots of male friends. I'm not going to write them off just because you want me to . . . be exclusive."

"Of course not. I know you have many friends. But I hope to be more than that."

Oh. Um. Now would be the time to tell him about your breakfast date, girlfriend. The one happening in, like, four point five hours.

I took a breath and opened my mouth to say, "About those other friends—" when his arm slid around my waist and he tilted his head down and kissed me.

And I totally forgot my words.

chapter 10

DESPITE THE FACT that I don't drink anything stronger than Mountain Dew, and Rashid doesn't drink at all, when my phone rang at some horrific hour the next morning, I could hardly see to answer it. Was there such a thing as date hangover?

"Glmph?"

"Shani? Hello?"

"Guhh."

"Shani, it's Danyel. Are you okay?"

"Uhhh-huh."

"Are we still on for breakfast?"

I tilted the phone's bright face toward me: 7:57. Was that morning? Duh, breakfast. Of course it was morning. "What day is it?"

"It's Sunday. We were supposed to have breakfast at my sister's and go to church together, remember? I'm outside waiting for you. Are you sure you're okay?"

My mind processed these facts with all the speed of a glacier careening across a continent. "Oh. Right. Yeah, I'm okay. I just didn't get much sleep."

I'd lain awake in the dark for a long time, listening to Carly's and Mac's even breathing and thinking about Rashid's kiss. He'd made it crystal clear he wanted to take our friendship to the next level, and that kiss had given me a hint of what it could be like. I mean, I never thought I'd be in danger of being swept away by a guy, but that shows you what I know. I felt like I was standing on a stone above a waterfall, looking out at the rushing torrent that would claim me if I took a single step.

The problem was, there were people on this side of the river, too. People I wanted to stay with just as much.

Danyel cleared his throat. "So, are we on or do you want to skip?"

The words might have been cool, but underneath them was the rough sound of hurt. He'd expected me to be as glad to see him—as prepared, and yeah, like, dressed—as he clearly was to see me. He'd driven all the way up from Daly City to Pacific Heights to pick me up. Until two days ago, I'd been crushing on him to the point of telling him about it, and now what? Was I just going to hang up and go back to sleep because I'd been out too late with another guy?

Of course not. The only step I was going to take this morning was through the door in Spencer's foyer. "I'll be down in fifteen minutes. Don't leave."

"Not happening." The smile was back in his voice, and I felt a little better as I snapped the phone shut and rolled out of bed.

Luckily I'd showered, uh, four hours ago, so I could skip that part. And I'd only had the extensions put in two weeks before, so no hair worries. I splashed my face with water as cold as I could make it run and woke up enough to make a coherent decision on what to wear.

A skirt, not too short. My new Philip Lim 3.1 tuxedo shirt with the ruffled cuffs. A bright silk vest over it that Mom had sent from Paris in the summer, after she'd been to someone's trunk sale on the Left Bank.

Shoes. Hmm. I considered my inventory and thought, what would Lissa do? The girl always looks fabulous but she's practical, too. She wouldn't let Gillian go to this big sci-fi trade show in heels because her feet would have committed suicide by the end of it. Since I didn't know what was going on today, I decided on boots—my Sergio Rossi suedes with what Carly calls "swashbuckles" on the sides.

Speaking of . . . I glanced to my right. Mac blinked at me over her mound of covers.

"Oh, look." She yawned. "A roommate. Have we met?"

"Very funny. I went out last night—"

"We noticed," Carly said as she surfaced, too.

"—and forgot that Danyel was coming at eight to pick me up." I flipped open my phone: 8:13. "Gotta go."

"Aren't you coming with us?" Carly asked as I scooped up my roomy Helena de Natalio tote and tossed the phone into it.

"Danyel's taking me to his sister's and I'ma go to church with them." A final check in the mirror and I was good to go.

"Fill us in later," Carly said, a little hesitantly.

Guilt poked me, right under my heart. Okay, so I hadn't been around much yesterday, but we'd spent all Friday evening having an adventure together, hadn't we? And she knew me. It wasn't like I was Party Central with every club in town on speed dial.

"You know it," I promised, and hit the door at a run.

BLAME IT ON sleep deprivation. Or the fact that I'd told Danyel I liked him and then gone and kissed someone else. Whatever. Because breakfast was Awk. Ward.

Malika passed me a bowl of applesauce. "Try this on your pancakes, Shani. I made it myself. Our backyard is only big enough to hold one tree, but it produces enough for a whole orchard."

I took the bowl. "You made this?"

Danyel's brother-in-law Sol smiled at his wife as if she spun the thread to make their clothes, too. "What, you think applesauce only comes in cans?"

"I don't think anybody thinks that." Even I could hear the stiffness in my tone. But hey, did we really need the putdown this early on a Sunday morning? Before church?

"He was just teasing," Danyel murmured beside me. "Ease up."

Ease up? It wasn't me dissing people I'd just met. I handed him the applesauce and poured syrup on my pancake instead.

"You'll be hungry halfway through service, you don't eat more than that," Malika said. "How about some seven-grain toast?"

"She made that, too," Sol put in.

"No, thank you."

Malika smiled, too, though her eyes were busy sizing up Danyel and me and speculating on just what I was to her brother. She could speculate all she wanted. Even I didn't know the answer to that.

"You on a diet, girl? You don't look big enough to cast a shadow on a hot day, but who knows with girls now. It's all about that top-model nonsense."

"I never watch that show." *Project Runway*, now, that was different. But mostly I just listened while I did homework. She was the one taking notes.

"How's Rose doing after her first month of kindergarten?" Danyel changed the subject as he handed half a banana to his niece, who, I have to admit, was about as cute as kids came.

And they were off and running on the fascinating subjects of finger painting and the alphabet, leaving me in peace to eat my pancake—I hate them, did I tell you?—and steal a couple of eggs off the plate when no one was paying attention.

After breakfast, church turned out to be a relief. Danyel's family visited over their shoulders with people as we all settled into the pew, but no one said much to me—though somehow the pastor figured I should be going with the youth group to do whatever they did. I just looked at him and stayed planted where I was, and he got on with it. The service wasn't like the one at Lissa's church in Marin. Instead, it was more like the one I'd gone to with Gram as a kid. I even knew some of the songs, and got a little of the spirit as I let my voice go. Malika watched me out of the corner of her eye, her eyebrow raised just enough to tell me I'd surprised her.

Huh. Yeah, I can sing. That probably doesn't make up for not liking your pancakes, though. Or for liking your brother.

". . . and Mary's chosen the better part," the pastor said, "and she's sitting at the feet of Jesus, listening to what He says."

I tuned in. The pastor was pretty interesting. There was nothing wrong with what Martha was doing with all her housekeeping and serving and homemade applesauce. Somebody had to keep the place clean with a dozen dusty guys overrunning it. But there was Mary, ticking off her sister because she'd rather listen to Jesus than help with the dishes.

Yeah, no kidding. I'd be right there with Mary, too. I mean, if a person gets the choice, it seems like a no-brainer, right? How else is a person supposed to learn?

After a couple more songs, during which I watched Danyel's fingers move as he held the hymnbook—I don't think he realized he was doing the chord changes—the service let out.

"You're coming back for lunch, right?" Malika said. Then she leaned to look behind the seat of his truck. "Why's your stuff in here?"

"I don't think so, Mal. I've got to take Shani up to the city and drop her off, then head south. School tomorrow."

"The BART station's only ten minutes from here. Why don't you two stay and eat and then you can drop Shani there?"

Oh, happy thought. Just what I wanted—to be dropped off at the train station like a suitcase. This woman did not like me, and that was that. Carly was so lucky. Brett's parents thought she walked on water. She got hugs every time she went over, and his mom had given her an all-access pass to the fabric stash from Italy.

What do I get? Botulism in a bowl and BART.

"Thanks, Mal, but I want to take Shani back. We don't get a lot of time to just talk."

"You can talk here."

"Sis." He gave her a hug that meant good-bye. "Leave it."

She hugged him back. "Can't blame a sister for trying. It's not like we see you every weekend."

"I'll try to get up here more often." He hugged Sol, and gave little Rose a big, smacking kiss that made her giggle and hide behind her mama's (no doubt homemade) dress. "Come on, Shani."

Okay, so maybe botulism was a little harsh. The applesauce probably only had a touch of salmonella. Which was completely survivable.

Danyel didn't say anything until we were on 101 heading north and completely free of little blue signs pointing the way to the BART station. "You okay?"

"Sure."

"You just seem kinda tense, that's all."

"I'm fine."

"My sister means well. She's a nutritionist and the kitchen is kind of her lab. When we were kids she'd grind up all kinds of seeds and pods and make me eat them. I used to envy the guys whose sisters made mud pies."

My chilly frontal shield melted and I laughed. "At least Rose will be healthy."

"She'll turn thirteen and her big rebellion will be to blitz out on Fritos and Red Bull."

"With a side of Twinkies and a bag of Gummi Worms." It felt good to laugh with him. "Sorry, Danyel. Maybe I should send Malika an e-mail saying I actually do like applesauce."

He tipped his head in acknowledgement. "Next time you'll feel more comfortable."

"You want to inflict me on your family again?"

"Sure. Malika owes me for years of abuse." He looked so happy about it.

"I always wondered what it would be like to have a sib."

"You an only?"

I nodded. "An only that wasn't in the plan." He looked puzzled, his eyes on the freeway, so I went on. "I mean, my folks didn't mean to have kids. Oh, they took good care of me. Their house is in an upscale neighborhood, I've been to the best schools, and have anything I want. But I only see them on layovers, it seems like. And if there's some big school event, I have to give them, like, a month's notice."

"I've heard of people's dads having jobs like that, but your mom does, too?"

"She goes with him everywhere, when she's not chairing charity events in Chicago. She sends me e-mail from places like Cairo and Paris. The last one was from London. She saw a picture on the Web and was all squee about it."

"What picture?"

I gave my guilty self a mental smack and waved a careless hand, as if it didn't matter. "A bunch of us were out at TouTou's and the paparazzi were there. Mom must have a Google alert on Spencer or something. Keeps her up on what I'm doing."

He snorted. "That's cold."

"Sometimes I think it's easier for her to be my mom over e-mail than it is in person." I shrugged. "Anyway, they expect Big Things. Whether I buy into it or not."

"What kind of big things?"

"I want to run my dad's company some day. But I think it's more than that. Mom's all up in my social life right now. That's never happened before." Probably because I'd never dated a prince before.

"Maybe she misses you. And like you say, this is her way to connect."

"It's a little late for that. I'll be eighteen in October and then it's hello, Stanford."

"If you get in."

"Right. Along with the Farm, I'm applying to Harvard Business School, plus Northwestern, Pepperdine, and Sarah Lawrence."

"Wow. Ambitious much?"

"Aren't you?"

"Maybe, but in a different way. I was thinking of taking a year off and going to Brazil or Africa to help our missions. And then when I get back, I'll apply to Stanford Law or Harvard Law."

"You're going to be a lawyer? How are you going to catch the waves when you're holed up in the law library with glasses on your head?"

He grinned and swung left on California Street. "That would be the advantage of Stanford. Santa Cruz is only an hour away. And lots of environmental lawyers surf. It's like a job requirement."

"It is?"

"No, but I could start a trend."

We laughed together at the visual, but at the same time, I had a lot to chew on. My dad's company went exploring for oil. He had a subsidiary that cleaned up the sites afterward, but you had to believe the birds and animals in the ecosystems weren't exactly beating a path back there. And Danyel would be dedicated to saving those ecosystems. Someday, in a far gray future, would he and I be on opposite sides of some courtroom? Would we look at each other and remember we once sat on a sunset beach and sang old songs around a fire? Or would we have forgotten each other's names by then?

Man. Here I was, riding in a Jeep with one of the hottest and nicest boys I'd met in the past decade, and what was I doing? Taking an E-ticket ride straight to the blues.

He jammed the Jeep into low gear to take the last hill, and before I could come up with some cheery conversation starter, we were cruising through the school gates past two photographers hunched into their jackets, and pulling to a stop in front of the steps.

"I wish I didn't have to drive away." Danyel set the emergency brake, even though the driveway was flat. "Seems like I'm always having to say good-bye before I'm ready."

"There's still phone and e-mail. And you promised your sister you'd be back soon."

He gave me a long look. "What did you think of their church?"

I picked up my bag and pretended to check that everything was in it. "It was good. Your pastor makes sense. Some of them don't. They're so far above my head, they can't see where I'm coming from. But this guy was okay."

"Think you'd like to go again?"

"Danyel." I closed my bag. "Stop pressuring me."

"I'm not. I just hate to see anyone not enjoying the ride through life with my big bro Jesus, that's all."

"I'm enjoying the ride just fine."

"You say that."

"I mean it. What's with you, anyway? Gillian and Lissa and Carly never bug me about it. They do stuff like prayer circle, and I go and it's all normal. They don't ask me what did I think."

"Maybe I'm more invested than they are."

"What does that mean?"

He ran his hands over the steering wheel, making two halves of a circle. "Honestly?"

"I wouldn't have it any other way."

"The Bible says we're not supposed to be unequally yoked with unbelievers. But besides that, if I was going out with a girl, it's just easier if we both have the same expectations."

"About what?"

He shrugged. "The physical side, for one thing."

I flashed on Rashid's kiss last night—er, early this morning. "Why, did you make a promise like Lissa did? Do guys do that, too?"

"Sure. And yeah."

"So I can live with that. I can wear white to a wedding, if you know what I mean."

He chuckled. "TMI, but thanks for telling me."

"So now that we have that cleared up, what else?"

"You sound like you're negotiating."

"I *feel* like I'm negotiating. So what you're saying is we can't date unless I go to church?"

"No way. What I'm saying is a relationship is . . . more when you both believe. You can share more."

"You had this with your other girlfriends?"

"One. I've done it both ways. That's how I know."

"What happened?"

He lifted a shoulder. "We were sophomores. We moved on. Mostly I just have friends now and don't get too serious. Then I went to this beach party at a friend's and all that blew up." His grin held all the promise a girl could want. It could make her do something crazy, like go to church every Sunday because it was something she wanted and needed instead of just a thing to do with her friends.

I gripped the door handle and steadied myself. If I did that, what was I going to do about Rashid? I mean, you have seven-grain toast and surfboards on one hand, and front-row seating and stretch limousines on the other. Dark eyes and being treated like a princess versus dark eyes and being treated like a . . . what? A friend with possibilities? A practice Christian?

Rashid thought I was amazing just the way I was. Danyel thought I could be amazing with a little work.

On the other hand, I was attracted to both of them, in different ways. With Danyel, I could show up in a headwrap and a layer of moisturizer and he wouldn't bat an eye—he'd just offer me something to eat, and talk. With Rashid, I could be the girl my parents wanted me to be—the glittering socialite mixing with all the best crowds.

Which was me? What did I want? *Who* did I want?

Because this couldn't go on forever, partying with Rashid Saturday night and going to church with Danyel Sunday morning. I had to make up my mind before one of them found out about the other.

Which, knowing the grapevine at Spencer, was only a matter of time.

Celebrity Hangout Shuts Down

Pacific Heights hot spot TouTou's is officially off the party circuit. According to charges filed this week, the restaurant owners, members of a local corporation, face several counts of serving alcohol to minors.

One employee, a member of the waitstaff who refused to be named for this article, said that it was
common practice for the private rooms upstairs to be
reserved for parties, where underage guests were freely
served everything from beer to martinis. "The management knew all about it," he said in a telephone interview. "But those kids made it worth his while."

While the employee declined to name names for fear
of retaliatory lawsuits, it's common knowledge among
the party set that students from Spencer Academy
have been using TouTou's as their personal venue from
which to see and be seen. Whether they were among
those minors being served is unclear.

What is clear is that local celebs will have to find another place to go on their off nights. A sign has already
been posted on the restaurant's door advising the public that it has been closed indefinitely.

A preliminary hearing has been scheduled for early
next week.

chapter 11

THE NEWS ABOUT TouTou's spread through the seniors like a grass fire. If I'd been Vanessa or Dani or DeLayne, I'd have been looking over my shoulder waiting for the cops to arrive, but they went to classes looking cool and unruffled. The most anyone got out of them was a bored, "We were tired of going there anyway. Have you heard about Cream? It's opening on Nob Hill and you have to be a member to get in."

Of course they were already members.

Rashid was, too. The always resourceful Bashir never failed to amaze me—just on the off chance that the prince might want to hang out with the rest of the A-list, he'd already gone down and intimidated the management into giving him a tier-one pass. Not that it mattered to me. But someday, when I was running PetroNova, I was going to have an assistant with those kinds of skills. Only he'd be cuter. And dress in something other than black suits.

"Are you getting into Cream?" I asked Carly on Tuesday morning on the way to Global Studies, which we had together.

I was still feeling a little ragged after my busy weekend, but it was nothing a little Mountain Dew couldn't cure. "And do you have any clue who squealed on TouTou's?"

"No and no," Carly said.

I stopped in the corridor and dragged her to the side, even though people seemed to be clearing a path for us. "What do you mean, no? Everybody's trying to get into Cream. It opens on Saturday. Rashid already has his pass."

"Of course he does." Carly shrugged. "Everybody can do what they want, but Brett and I discovered this totally cool gallery-slash-restaurant-slash-dance floor that's going to open in the Marina. His cousin owns it. It's like Second Life, only alive."

"Um, isn't that the point of Second Life? To not be alive?"

"You should see it. It's called Due." She pronounced it the Italian way, "doo-ay." "Every table has a flat screen embedded in it, and it makes an avatar of you when you sign in and sit down. Then if you want to ask someone to dance, you send your avatar over. If they turn you down, no harm, no foul. You can order and send drinks and food that way and everything."

"Huh." It did sound cool. "Do you have to be a member?"

"You swipe a card so they can activate your avatar, but it's not like Cream. I mean, stuffy much?"

I laughed. "Good point."

"It's just fun, you know? And I can use some fun right now."

"Why, what's going on?" She looked just the same. She'd pulled her hair straight back in a cute retro hair band, so her curls fell down her back, but that was about it.

"If you'd stick around for more than two seconds, you'd know. Mac and I got our subpoenas on Saturday."

"Oh, my gosh."

Carly began to walk down the corridor. In between smiles and people saying hey, she gave me the scoop. "David Nelson had his preliminary hearing in the summer, right? So we knew this was coming because he pleaded *not guilty*, if you can believe it. Mac and I have to testify next week."

"Are you scared?"

"Not really. Well, yeah, sort of. I never met the guy, just saw him from a distance. It's Mac I'm worried about."

"I can't see her being scared of anything."

"She is, though. Underneath. Her mom's coming, but I don't know how much that'll help."

"Wow. Good thing she has us."

Carly nodded as we went into our classroom. "And it's a good thing we have God."

Okay. Some of us had God, at least.

Did she have to bring that up?

VTalbot	Can't wait for Saturday. How's the guest list coming?
EOverton	Still working on it.
VTalbot	It's Tuesday. You should have it nailed down by now.
EOverton	Maybe you'd like to take care of it yourself?
VTalbot	At this rate I'll have to. How many solid? I want to make sure Cream has enough tables and their event planner is briefed.
EOverton	20.
VTalbot	You have to be kidding. What have you been doing all this time? Eating?
EOverton	We'll have 100 by Friday. Promise.

RASHID INCLINED HIS HEAD toward the table by the window, and Farrouk carried our plates over and set them down.

"Rashid," I said, "there's something you should know about this table."

"I have sat here many times." He pulled out a chair for me and waited.

"Yeah, when Vanessa invited you. No one sits here except her and her friends."

"No one tells the Prince of Yasir that he cannot sit here or there." He raised an eyebrow at the chair and then at me.

I sat. When Vanessa showed up, he could deal with her. Meanwhile . . . I waved as Brett and Carly put their plates down at a place across the room. And picked them up again. And walked over to us.

"Hey." Brett pulled out a chair for Carly and waited. Wow. Had Rashid been giving him lessons?

Carly hesitated and glanced at me. "You know we're not going to get away with this. I totally don't feel like a scene right now."

Mac joined us. "Tsk-tsk. Aren't we brave?"

"What are you two talking about?" Brett wanted to know.

"Vanessa and Emily and that crowd are going to kill us," Carly said. "You know it, I know it, and everyone in this room knows it."

Rashid frowned at her. "I think you overrate their importance."

"They aren't that bad," Brett said. "I'll protect you."

"I don't need protecting," I told him. "But you have to admit these tables are divided up by cliques. And Vanessa's has the most clout."

"Some of us don't care," Mac observed, picking up her hot prosciutto and Gruyère panini sandwich. "I say we give them a challenge."

"I say we're about to," Carly murmured. "Look who just walked in."

It had probably never occurred to Vanessa and her friends to pick a backup table in case theirs was full. In the nearly four years I've been going here, that has never happened, not even once. The A-list had their table by the window, and that was that—an immutable law of the universe, like gravity or photosynthesis.

So when they turned with their plates and saw us sitting there, chatting and laughing and pretending we hadn't seen them, the identical OMG faces were almost laughworthy.

"Rashid, Brett, how cool that you're joining us," Vanessa said, without wasting a single flick of an eyelash on any of us girls. Until she got to me. "Excuse me, you're sitting in my chair."

I straightened, ready to leap up and get in her face if I had to. *Vive la révolution.*

Rashid put his hand on my forearm. "I have invited Shani to sit here."

Vanessa's long-lashed brown eyes rested on me just long enough to convey the message that life as I knew it was over. Still, she couldn't argue with the fact that the prince was on the A-list by her invitation, and I was there by his. Her gaze tracked to Rashid's other side, where Carly took another bite of her panini and turned to Brett.

"These are really good. I got the cranberry and Brie one. What did you get?"

Carrying her plate, Vanessa walked around to Carly's chair while Emily and Dani Lavigne looked torn between eating their lunches standing up or pre-empting Vanessa's victory by pulling out the empty chairs in front of them. In any case, their sandwiches could only be getting cold.

Not that I was wasting any sympathy.

"Excuse me, Carolyn," Vanessa said. "I'd like to talk to Rashid. Privately." Carly took another bite and didn't answer. "Carolyn. Did you hear me?"

Carly swallowed and looked over her shoulder, surprised. "There's no one named Carolyn here. Who were you talking to?"

"You, obviously. I hate when people play stupid for effect."

"It's better than actually *being* stupid," Carly said, as though she and Vanessa were having a real conversation. "I know you know my name. It's cheap to pretend you don't."

I had a hard time keeping my jaw from hitting the glossy hardwood tabletop. Mac and I were one thing. I kinda had a rep for not mincing words, and Mac had no filters at all. But since when did Carly take on Spencer's social queen? And check out the 'tude. As in, none. She was as calm and cool as if they were discussing the insides of their sandwiches. More. At least with the sandwich, she sounded interested in the answer.

"It's cheap to pretend you didn't hear what I asked you," Vanessa retorted. "I want to sit there."

"That will make your situation at present more pitiable, but it will have no effect on me."

It took me a second to realize she was channeling Elizabeth Bennet. I bit my lip to keep from laughing and glanced across the table at Lissa, who had just done a hip swivel around Emily and taken the chair opposite Carly. Her face stayed expressionless, but I could clearly see *Go, girl!* in her dancing eyes.

"Give it a rest, Van," Brett said. "Pull up a chair if you want, but don't go kicking people out. That's subzero."

"Easy for you to say," she snapped. "I kicked you out months ago."

"Best thing that ever happened to me." He gave Carly the kind of smile that a girl can only dream about, and squeezed her shoulders.

"Hey Gillian, Jeremy," Carly said as they pulled up the chairs right in front of Emily and Dani and put their plates down. "Feel free to join us, Vanessa. There's a seat on the end, there. But it looks like Emily and Dani might have to go somewhere else."

"You snooze, you lose," Gillian said cheerfully, and bit into her sandwich. "Everyone ready for their thirdterms?"

Lissa and I jumped in with groans of dismay. Hey, I was prepped. I had a nasty paper to write for World Lit, but Lissa would help me with that. And calculus was never a picnic, but then, when is it ever for anyone?

"Dani, Emily, there's the rowing team," Vanessa said just loud enough to override us. "I'm ready for a change. Let's sit with people who are interesting, at least."

Emily looked from Rashid to Brett to the table where the rowing team was joshing and pushing and it looked like a food fight would break out any minute. Only the really brave sat with the jocks—when they weren't diluted by girls—because the risk was real. Then again, I'd bet on Vanessa against a whole boatload of jocks any day.

Emily reached for the chair on the end. "I—I think I'm going to stay here. I want to talk to Gillian about something."

"I already told you, I'm too busy to tutor," Gillian told her.

Emily looked crushed and kind of pale. "N-not about that."

"Whatever it is, you don't really need to know now," Vanessa said. "Come on."

Emily's spine wilted. "Okay."

The two of them trailed Vanessa over to the jocks' table, where they were greeted by a cheer. Someone affectionately stole Emily's sandwich and pretended to eat it. Since the poor kid is, um, spatially challenged, hinting that she didn't need it wasn't the most tactful thing to do. But no one's ever accused Tate and his jock buddies of being that evolved.

Lissa looked across the table at us. "What just happened?"

"They have found another place to eat." Maybe it was the language thing, or maybe Rashid took things literally all the time.

"Something's going on," I said. "Changes."

"We're sitting at the A-listers' table." Lissa repeated the

obvious as though she couldn't quite believe it. I half expected her to knock on it to make sure it was real. "Vanessa just gave up her table to us."

"I think she gave it up to Rashid and Brett," Gillian said. "Temporarily. Supper will be a different story. You watch."

"I fully intend to sit here at supper," Rashid put in. "Vanessa was kind enough to invite me to join her and her friends the first evening, so I will invite her to join me and mine."

"Not to backtalk you or anything," I said, "but she'll probably send someone to stake it out long before you get here. Like the rowing team."

"Not," Brett put in laconically. "I'm the captain. If I say don't, they won't. And we have crew down at Foster City this afternoon. If we get back before the doors close, that'll be a stretch."

Jeremy stood with his empty plate. "I've gotta go look up some stuff for my World Lit paper in the library. Hey, speaking of, Lissa, what's this about the Hearst medal?"

Her pale skin warmed to a flush. "Curzon called me into her office before core class today."

I looked from one to the other. "Curzon had news about the Hearst medal? And you didn't tell us, why?"

"I was going to as soon as I came in, but got sidetracked by drama."

Gillian hugged her from behind. "She's a finalist, guys! Ten people in the whole state and she's one of them!"

"What is this medal?" Rashid wanted to know, amid shrieks from Carly and me.

"It's only open to the Honors English classes," I explained breathlessly. "You have to write an essay on some horrific topic—ten thousand words. You might as well write a book."

"It felt like a book," Lissa admitted. "But it wasn't horrific. I did it on the literary tradition of courtship in dance and dialogue, starting with Jane Austen and ending with Helen Fielding."

"Like I said. Horrific." I could feel my face stretching into a grimace even as I joined the rest to hug her in congratulations. "So, where are we going to celebrate?"

"Due, of course," Lissa said. "Saturday night, eight o'clock. All of you must come. No exceptions. Dress code: Glam To The Max."

I looked at Rashid. Cream? Tier-one pass? Hello?

He was smiling at her. "I will have a limousine for all of us at the door at seven thirty." He glanced at Bashir, standing next to the window. "See to it."

Bashir nodded. Once.

"I already invited everyone in my English class," Lissa said. "Feel free to invite whoever you want. It's opening night—it'll be crazy and fun."

It was opening night at Cream, too, and I'd overheard DeLayne Geary raving about how they were going all out for Vanessa's party. Total media coverage. Maybe a Hollywood celebrity or two.

Two places. Two opening nights.

Would the real A-list party please stand up?

chapter 12

AT SUPPER, AS PROMISED, the rowing team did not show up until about 6:45. Fortunately, the doors hadn't been closed yet, so at least they got fed. But it meant Brett wasn't there to anchor our little group of social rebels, and Mac and I couldn't talk the others into making a point of it.

So Vanessa won Round 2.

She also won dinner with Rashid, who refused to take his plate over to where we were sitting. Well, I refused to stay there with him. I'm no dummy. I was going to have to endure an entire school year with Vanessa, whereas he'd be flitting off to the desert at the end of term, where none of us would ever see him again.

It's not like I'm afraid of her or anything, but you do the math.

"I insist you sit with me," he told me, putting a hand on my arm to stop me. "I command it."

Okay, I'm not a computer. I don't do commands well. I shook off his hand. "Just because you kissed me doesn't give you the right to command me. We're in America now."

"But I—"

"I'll see you later, Rashid."

"When later? In the common room after dinner?"

"No, I'ma go to prayer circle. I don't know when. Probably tomorrow in class."

"But Shani—"

I don't think it's proper protocol to turn your back on a prince and walk away. But I was so steamed that I did it anyway.

Command. Hmph.

And then all I got was a stomachache from stress—or maybe the faux Szechuan food Dining Services dished up did it. Gillian spent the dinner hour happily dissing their cooking skills while I watched Rashid practically cheek-to-cheek with Vanessa, no doubt discussing the finer properties of kinetic energy.

Snarl.

At prayer circle, Lissa came armed with her laptop, which made me perk up a little. Sure enough, Danyel had made another video of his prayer. For some reason, this calmed me down and I could focus on finding some peace instead of feeling all mad and jangly inside, like a band playing together for the first time who can't quite find the beat.

When my turn came, I hesitated. Now, normally I'd just smile and say, "Pass." Everyone's used to it, but they still pause for a second and wait, just because.

Next to me, Lissa waited the usual couple of seconds and then I heard her inhale.

"God?" I blurted, as much to my own surprise as everyone else's. "God, I have no idea if you're out there listening to me, but these guys say you are. They say that if I just talk to You, You'll answer. Okay. I'm talking. I'm dealing with a lot of stress and a lot of things are bugging me. If You can give me a hand with that, I'll be glad. Thanks." I paused. What did they say to wrap it up? Oh, yeah. "Amen."

It took Lissa a second to speak. I guess she was recovering from the surprise. Anyway, she swallowed and began to pray, and then Gillian and Carly followed her. When we were done, Carly came over and hugged me, hard.

"Kinda surprised, huh," I mumbled.

"Does this mean you want to give your life to God?" she asked.

"No!" I made "go away" motions with my hands. "*Nein. Non. Nada.* It doesn't mean anything. I need a little extra help, that's all, and you guys say this is the way to get it. I'm just giving it a try. Don't read anything into it."

"God might read something into it." Gillian was smiling like she knew something I didn't. Which, on every other subject, is probably true. "You might start something He's going to finish."

"I'll leave that up to Him." Time to change the subject. "Who's up for Starbucks?"

Gillian, Jeremy, and Lissa waved their hands. Carly shook her head. "I'm going to walk over to Brett's with him. His mom made zabaglione and wants us to eat most of it so she won't."

The four of us wandered down the hill in the twilight. It was still warm, but on the edges of the air, you could feel that fall was going to arrive any second. We were still two blocks from Starbucks when my phone rang.

"You guys go ahead. It's Danyel."

I flipped it open and leaned against a convenient garden wall cleverly designed to look as if it had been hand-chipped in Italy. "Hey. Didn't I just see you?"

His smile overflowed into his voice. "Lissa let me join you, huh? I never know if that girl is going to keep the lid on me or not."

"She'd never do that. It's kind of neat. You should get Kaz to do it, too."

"He's too shy."

"Why? Doesn't he pray in church?"

"Not that kind of shy. Whenever Lissa is in the room, shy takes on a whole new meaning."

"Uh-huh. When are you gonna sit that boy down and tell him that if he doesn't make his move, she's going to do something extreme—like date a jock. This guy named Tate is hanging around us way too much, and since Jeremy warned him off Gillian, and I know it's not for my benefit, and Mac won't give him the time of day, that leaves her."

"Ugh. Say it ain't so."

"She's not desperate, but she's not short of offers, either. I'm tellin' you, the risk is there."

He thought for a moment. "Can you keep a secret?"

"Do chickens have lips?"

"Uh, I'm guessing no."

"I'm bad at secrets. If they're good news, I want to share ASAP. If they're bad news, the person usually needs to know. So. Not good with secrets."

He laughed. "Okay, well, try to hang onto this one, will you? Kaz wants to come up there one of these weekends. So of course I'd ride shotgun."

"That'd be great. We'd love to see you."

"He's so happy about the Hearst medal, you'd think *he* was the finalist."

"Oh, I get it. It's totally just an excuse to see her."

"And it's totally just an excuse for me to see you. So, see? It'd work out for everyone."

I laughed while my stomach did a nosedive into my Miu Miu flats. "You're not thinking *this* weekend, are you?"

He didn't seem to hear the edge in my tone. Thank goodness for the missing bar on my cell phone's reception. "That would mean we actually had a plan. I don't know. Kaz told

Gillian sometime soon, though. I mean, he'd better do something before they announce the winner, right?"

"Right." *Breathe. Whew.* "But wait. Kaz told Gillian? Isn't he talking to Lissa, like, on a daily basis?"

"I think he called to say congrats when the list came out, but he doesn't want to smother her." He paused. "So, who's Rashid?"

"Guhhh, what?"

"Did you just walk under a power line? I said, who's Rashid? Gillian said he was the new face in town. I figure he has to be one of your trust fund types."

"Yeah, he's a real prince."

Danyel laughed. "And you're still hanging out with him?"

"I wouldn't say we were hanging out." Making out, maybe. I pressed a hand to my hot face. I had to end this conversation. "But he's nice enough. Listen, Danyel, I have to go. Everyone's waiting for me."

"No problem. See you soon, I hope."

"Me, too."

I hung up and sucked in a big breath of air. *Calm. Breathe. Think.*

First order of business: Impress upon Gillian that there were certain subjects that needed to stay off-limits. And my connection with Rashid was one of them.

Second order: Make up my inconsistent, treacherous, two-timing mind and decide which guy I was going out with.

Before Danyel turned up when I least expected it.

GChang   Zao, surfing tiger.

KazG   Hey, jumping loon. Wassup?

GChang   Got plans for this weekend?

KazG	Are you kidding? Me and Danyel have a wild weekend ahead of doing exactly what we do every weekend. Missing y'all and surfing.
GChang	There's a new place opening on Saturday. Check out fordue.com. We're all going in a limo. Would be totally fun if you guys came.
KazG	Lissa's going?
GChang	Duh. Her, me, Jeremy, Shani, Mac, Brett, Rashid. And his bodyguards, but they're kind of invisible.
KazG	Hm. Could make it by 9 if we left right after school.
GChang	Don't tell. It'll be a surprise for Lissa.
KazG	Got it. See you there.
GChang	Dress code's glam.
KazG	Danyel does glam. I do glum.
GChang	No glums allowed. We're celebrating. At least wear clean jeans.

IT TOOK RASHID a couple of days to get over my lack of obedience training. On Thursday afternoon after classes were over he found me on the front lawn in the sun, my World Lit books scattered around me.

"There you are." As if he hadn't been ignoring me for half the week, he folded himself onto the grass, pulling a fat old tome of literary theory out from under his hip. I appeared to have been forgiven. "What are you working on?"

"Midterm paper." Where was that paragraph I'd marked in Nalo Hopkinson's *The Salt Roads*? What insanity had made me decide that a paper on the connection between love and immortality in Caribbean myth was a good idea? And most important of all, how was I going to get this done before class on Monday? Friday afternoon was devoted to manicures and massages, Saturday was hair and makeup, and Sunday was recovery. Nobody could expect anything out of me until at least two o'clock—especially homework.

"Stop now and—" Rashid checked himself. "Please take a break from your work. I would like to talk to you."

I had to give the guy credit. He was willing to swallow his royal habits and relate to me like an ordinary person. The least I could do was talk to him. "Okay. But only for a minute. I seriously have to get some of this written today. I don't want it bugging me while I'm trying to have fun getting ready for the party Saturday."

"It is the party I want to talk about."

"Oh. Well, then. Why didn't you say so?" I grinned at him, sat back on my hands, and then a thought struck me. "You didn't change your mind and decide to go to Cream, did you?" That would mean that underneath, he was really mad at me and I'd have to do some serious kissing up to get back in his good books.

Not because I was shallow and liked hanging out with royalty. But because he was my friend, and it left me feeling hollow inside when my friends were mad at me. If I was going to go to Due with him, I wanted everything to be cool between us.

He shook his head. "But I realized I did not actually ask you to go with me. It is all very well to do these things as a group of friends, but that is no longer enough for me."

"Of course I'll go with you." I'd figure out how to explain it to Danyel later. Or . . . hey. Maybe that was the answer. Maybe Danyel needed to know I'd been with someone else to light a fire under his fine behind. Maybe that would make him unload this fixation on me having to be someone I wasn't yet—and goose him past "just friends" to "boyfriend."

"I had hoped you might say that." Rashid smiled, a slow, intimate smile that, okay, made my temperature rise a couple of degrees. Was I conflicted or what? I wanted Danyel because of who he was, and I wanted Rashid because of how he made me feel. And how he might make Danyel feel. As in, jealous.

That's pretty low. First of all, Rashid is your friend. How's he going to feel when he finds out you want to use him like that?

Well, when you put it that way . . . I wished they'd flip. I wanted Rashid thinking in "just friends" mode and Danyel thinking in "boyfriend" mode. But they were just the opposite.

Having two guys on the hook was a lot harder and more complicated than I'd ever thought it would be.

Meanwhile, Rashid waited patiently for me to say something. "I have to confess, I kind of took it for granted we were going as a couple, even if I made you mad this week," I said. "Guess I would have looked the fool, huh?"

"I am not, as you say, mad. And you will never look foolish on my account." He sounded as if that was about to be written into parliamentary law, back there in Yasir. "In fact, if you will allow me, the opposite will be true."

How intriguing. "What do you mean?"

"You have several big events coming up in the next weeks, yes?"

I counted off on my fingers. "Sure. Saturday night, for one. The movie premiere. The annual Christmas shindig the school holds to support the San Francisco Ballet School. And that doesn't even count stuff like graduation."

"And you will need things to wear to all of these."

I laughed. "Like I need air to breathe. What are you getting at, Rashid?"

He reached into the inner pocket of his school blazer and pulled out a flat, narrow velvet box. On the top I glimpsed an H and a W, set in a cartouche.

Oh.

My.

G—

"I would be honored if you would accept this and wear it to these events."

Harry Winston. That couldn't be a Harry Winston box. No way. He was using it to hold something else, like a charm bracelet he'd gotten down at the wharf, with "I ♥ San Francisco" and little Golden Gate Bridges dangling from it.

He tilted back the lid, and it would have taken the threat of death for me not to look.

Nestled in black velvet was a diamond necklace.

And not just any necklace. A diamond cluster necklace from the latest collection, with a big yellow stone dangling from the center. It had to have been custom-made, because that stone hadn't been on any of the fashion Web sites. And none of the pieces in the new collection had appeared in any of the magazines yet—only customers like my mother had had advance previews.

I dragged my gaze off it, looked up at Rashid, and sat on my hands so they wouldn't grab. At him or the necklace, I wasn't sure.

"Who is this for?" I finally managed out of a throat that threatened to close up altogether.

"It is for you. Don't you like it?"

"Anyone would be insane not to like it. It's the most beautiful thing I've ever seen."

"Then why are you not putting it on?" He tilted slightly to the left, lifting an amused eyebrow at my hands, flattened on the grass under my thighs.

"Because it can't be for me."

"I assure you it is. It was delivered into the hands of Farrouk on Monday in New York."

"You sent the poor guy all the way to New York to get this?"

"It would have come from London, but the gentleman who prepares my mother's pieces was on his way to Cabo San Lucas and agreed to meet halfway."

Okay, I was seriously dreaming. I turned one hand over and pinched it.

Ow. Not dreaming.

Not accepting reality very well, either.

I gave the necklace's pretty pear-shaped clusters one last hungry look and released my hands from prison long enough to close the box and push it toward Rashid. "Of course I can't accept this."

"Of course you can. I ordered it for you. You will look like the princess in the fairy tale."

"No. I'm serious. Even if you weren't richer than Bill Gates squared, I couldn't take it. This isn't a fairy tale. It's serious— the kind of thing a guy gives his fiancée. And we aren't even going out. I'm nothing to you except a little girl you played with on a beach. Our *mothers* are closer than we are."

Slowly, his face changed from "Look what I did—aren't you delighted?" to "Oh my gosh, she really means it." I hoped the necklace was returnable to the gentleman in Cabo.

My hands still tingled with the urge to rip the box out of his hands and run away with it, but I stood my ground. Well, technically, I sat my ground.

Get up, Shani. Walk away from the pretty sparklies.

Rashid looked so disappointed that I reached out and touched his hand. His pride I had no problem stepping on. But a person's feelings mattered, and it had taken him—and Farrouk—considerable time to do this. Not to mention expense. My brain couldn't even go there. I spoke as gently as I could. "This necklace is what you give a girl at the end of the—the, um, courtship. When you decide to get married. Not at the beginning, when you've only had two dates."

"You are special to me," he said softly. "This is how I must express it. You are not just the little girl on the beach. You are the friend who has made my time away from home bearable. Even when you are angry, you have been a friend to me when others have been—how do you say it?—only suckups." We grinned at a word like that coming out of his mouth. "This gift holds my thanks for your friendship, and my hopes that someday it might be more."

Something in my hard little heart melted, just on the very edges, and the heat of it sent a blush into my face. "Rashid, I—I can't promise you more."

"I know it is very soon. But I wanted you to know of my hopes."

I couldn't speak. This was way more serious than a couple of dates and a kiss. This was that river, back in full force. I couldn't walk into it and come out intact.

"May I make a suggestion?" he asked gently, when the silence filled with traffic noises and birdsong and me not talking.

I looked up. "Sure."

"Will you wear the necklace on Saturday night, simply as a loan from a friend? It would please me very much."

I opened my mouth to say no, and stalled as a visual filled the screen of my mind. Dancing at Due, sparkling in the single most expensive object I or any of my friends had ever worn. Well, okay, with the possible exception of the eighteenth-century tiara that Mac had tucked away in her mom's bank vault. Maybe we'd even drop in at Cream so Vanessa could get an eyeful of it. Call me shallow, but I wanted to step out of my self-imposed shell and show those people I was someone, that I had friends to whom I mattered. That I wasn't an island anymore.

I blinked and focused on Rashid. "Just Saturday night. And then I give it back to you and you give it back to the, er, gentleman in Cabo."

"Agreed."

"Rashid, for a prince, you make a really nice guy."

He laughed and leaned over to kiss me on the cheek. As he did, he slipped the narrow velvet box into the pocket of my jacket. "Keep this safe."

"I will." Duh. I wondered if Ms. Curzon had an underground bunker I could keep it in.

"And now I must go beat Tate DeLeon, who has been foolish enough to challenge me to a game of squash." He got up, nodded at Bashir and Farrouk, who were pretending to be garden statues, and walked across the lawn in the direction of the field house.

Leaving me with a couple of million in diamonds in my school jacket.

I waited until he was safely out of sight, then scooped up all my books and threw them into my bag. The velvet box bumped gently against my hip as I ran into the building, up three flights of stairs, and down the corridor into my room.

Carly and Mac jumped about a foot as the door bounced off the wall and slammed itself shut behind me.

"Shani!" Carly squeaked. "What happened to you?"

I tossed my bag on the floor so that it skidded across the parquet and fetched up against my bed. "You will not believe—" I managed to gasp, and ran for the bathroom with its four-foot mirror.

With shaking hands, I twisted my corkscrew spirals up—*gotta get rid of these first thing and lay on the relaxers*—into an approximation of a roll and clipped it in place. Then I stripped off my jacket and uniform blouse. Carly and Mac crowded into the bathroom behind me, concern times two crowding in along with them.

"Are you all right?" Mac demanded. "Have you gone utterly mad?"

Standing in only my plaid skirt and lace cami, I pulled the box out of my jacket pocket and opened it. Carly leaned in and gasped.

Mac squawked a Scottish expletive about some saint on a tricycle in frilly pantaloons.

The necklace slid over my shaking fingers in a cool, sparkling caress as I held it up to my throat. "Somebody do it up," I whispered.

Mac fastened the clasp, her own fingers ice-cold against the back of my neck.

"Where . . . how . . . ?" Carly couldn't get a sentence started. Her eyes had widened to perfect circles as she gawked at me.

I didn't try to answer. Every cell in my body was focused on the image in the mirror.

I lifted my chin and dropped my shoulders.

Long, smooth neck.

Cream lace against coffee skin, and lying on it, the frozen fire of all those diamonds. The big yellow one lay dead center, looking as though it were gaining warmth from my body with every second.

Rashid was right. I looked like a princess.

That two-timing Dana Douglas

She has one husband in the 18th century. Another in the 21st. And they have more in common than she knows.

The Middle Window

Lucasfilm and Blade Productions request the honor of your presence at the premiere of their film, *The Middle Window*, at the Kodak Theatre in Hollywood, California, on November 21, 2009.

6:00 p.m.   Social hour. Red carpet opens.

8:00 p.m.   Film premiere.

11:00 p.m. Afterparty hosted by stars Cameron Diaz and Ewan McGregor, poolside at the Chateau Marmont.

Dress: Black tie.

RSVP: mwrsvp@bladeprdns.com or 310-555-2750

We look forward to sharing our first collaboration with you.

George and Gabriel

chapter 13

THE INVITATIONS to the premiere came by messenger on Friday, just in time for half the school to be passing through the reception hall on their way to the dining room. So naturally everyone heard us squeeing and waving them around and generally giving everyone something to talk about for the rest of the evening.

Heh.

We didn't bribe the messenger, I promise.

I hadn't realized just how far the news had gone until I was hangin' in the common room the next day, flipping through the latest issue of *WWD* and waiting for the rest of the girls to get themselves together for our mani/pedi afternoon. I was quite happy with nothing in my head but the latest designs from Alexander McQueen when Rory Stapleton plunked his sorry self down on the couch next to me.

What, had The Bad Place frozen over and all the little demons gone skating?

"Hey." He grinned at me like all I'd ever wanted was this precious moment between us. "I want to talk to you."

I slapped the magazine shut and rolled it up, just in case. "What?"

"Would you relax? I don't bite."

"Yeah. You do. You totally bite."

He laughed as if I'd said something hilarious. "So. Howzigoin'?"

"Fine. Whatsitoya?"

Again with the laugh. He sounded like Eeyore on a good day. "You're such a funny chick."

"Dude. I have to go. What do you want?"

"How's the prince?"

"I don't know. Haven't seen him since yesterday, when we were all in American Diplomacy. That's, like, a class. Do you go to those, or do you just buy a grade off the Net?"

He waited until I was done. I don't think he even heard me. "So you guys aren't, like, official?"

"How is that any of your business?"

He shrugged, still grinning. "I wouldn't want to get a rep as a poacher, that's all. A man has his pride."

I stared at him. What did that have to do with me? "Bottom line, Rory." Ugh. I'd never voluntarily said his name. It felt like oil in my mouth.

"Bottom line is, I wondered if you had a date for the Cream gig tomorrow."

Lucky thing I was leaning on the arm of the couch. Otherwise I would have fallen right off it and sprawled on the floor. "Why would I be going to Cream? And why would you ever think I'd go with you?"

"Great, you don't have a date. I've got a tier-one pass." He lifted his arms and did a disgusting shimmy with his hips, which made his shirt pull out of his waistband, which made him look even more of a mess than he was. "We can dance, drink, get nasty. Huh? I figure you're a woman with taste.

If a guy's gotta have someone's seconds, it might as well be royalty."

I stared at him for a moment. Had he really said what I thought he'd said?

No. He couldn't have.

The grin slid sideways off his face. "What's the matter? You only date black guys?"

With all this offensiveness, I hardly knew where to begin. Maybe I should do like Lissa, and make a list. I stood up, clutching the rolled-up magazine. "One, you better not mean what I think you mean by *seconds*. Two, I date people I like, no matter what color they are. And three, I would rather date a Gila monster and go swimming in a live volcano than go out with you."

It took him a second to process this much information. Then his eyebrows went up. "You like swimming? We could go to the beach."

"No. Not now. Not ever."

"But me and Brett are buds. You and MexiDog are buds. That's, like, a foursome. You should try me on. You might like me."

I leaned into his face, and when his gaze dipped to my chest, the rat, I grabbed his chin and yanked it up. "Do. Not. Ever. Call her that in front of me."

"Uh. Okay. Hurting." As soon as I let go, he said, "So is it true you gave it up for the prince?"

"What?" I lost it and walloped him upside the head with *WWD* so hard he didn't even have the sense left to yell. "Go ahead, say that again!" I shrieked, and whapped him a second time. He threw himself over the back of the couch, but I didn't stick around to get the satisfaction of seeing him cowering on the floor. I hit the door and stomped across the entry hall, every slap of my jeweled flip-flops sounding like the smack of a hand on a face.

I looked up at a commotion on the stairs, and what a

relief—there were my girls. "You guys are gonna have to wait," I said. "I need a shower."

"What happened?" Carly looked me up and down. "Are you okay? Did you spill something?"

"No. Rory Stapleton asked me out. And then he insulted me to the power of a hundred."

Shrieks of disgust bounced off the floors, the stone pots with their palm trees, and the row of French windows opening onto the quad. They probably also bounced off the side of Rory's head, since he was still in the common room, but I didn't care. "I took care of him. He won't be opening his nasty mouth again. Let's get out of here."

We made wicked fun of the stupid nimnul all the way into Cow Hollow in the cab, which meant my happy levels were nearly back to normal by the time we flocked into the bamboo lobby of the Tea House.

After we'd chosen our colors (Rajah Ruby was going to go so well with the vintage Lanvin dress Gillian and I had scored in New York over the summer) we all settled into the leather chairs. Gillian winced as the aesthetician began to work on her cuticles. "I hate to bring up the creep again, but what made Rory ask you out? It's not like we're all kissy with that crowd to start with. I haven't heard word one about you being on his radar."

"Please don't let *that* rumor get started," I groaned. "That's even more disgusting than people thinking I'm sleeping with Rashid."

"No kidding," Gillian said. "I don't know how Brett can stand him."

"He can't," Carly said, her head back on the cushion and her eyes closed. "They were friends up until the exam-answer debacle last year, and then it was over."

Lissa snorted. "I was surprised to see him back here,

personally. But then I noticed the new Media Communications Center."

"The Lawrence Stapleton Bail-out and Guilt Center, you mean?" Gillian inquired. "With the brand-new, state-of-the-art workstations, editing booth, and professional video cameras?"

"That would be the one."

"Must be nice to have your dad bribe the headmistress to keep you in school." I shook my head.

"He'd have come back somehow. This way, Curzon gets a shiny new media lab at no cost to her," Lissa pointed out.

"At some cost to us, though," Carly said. "We have to put up with him for another nine months."

"I'm not putting up with him at all." At the aesthetician's prompting, I changed feet, submerging my left in the hot jets of the tub. "I'd never tell Rashid what he said, but if he comes near me again, I'll set Farrouk on him. That man carries a girl's best friend—a stun gun."

"From what I hear, a girl's best friend is locked in Curzon's safe," Lissa said. "I can't believe you didn't wait long enough to show me and Gill the ice."

"Too much exposure to all that compressed carbon can't be good for you," Gillian informed her. "It's better off behind lead."

"You'll see it tomorrow," I said.

"Everyone within a mile's radius will see it," Mac said. She'd been so quiet since we'd arrived that I wondered what was wrong. Maybe tonight when we were getting ready for bed, Carly and I would pry it out of her. "And you'll notice we've not said a word about why a man would be giving you such a thing?"

"He isn't giving it to me. I told you that yesterday, before we took it down to Curzon."

"Did she faint?" Lissa wanted to know.

"I didn't open the box. I just said it was a necklace and she put it away. The fewer people who know it's here, the better, right? Especially since it won't be around for long. I'm giving it back to Rashid on Sunday and it's going back to where it came from."

"So you guys aren't, like, engaged or anything," Gillian asked in her just-being-sure voice.

"Give me a break." I rolled my eyes at her.

"Because, you know, a guy doesn't drop a cool two million on just any *chica* in stilettos," Carly said.

"I'm wearing it once, then back it goes," I repeated firmly. "He's a prince. For all I know, he gives diamond earrings to his cleaning lady and sapphire bracelets to his teachers."

"Tobin would be happy about that," Carly said. "Hey, did you guys hear she and Mr. Milsom are getting married?"

"Ewww!" A chorus of noise made all our aestheticians look at us as though we'd lost our minds. "How do you know?"

"She has a quarter-carat diamond on her finger. I happened to be using a magnifying glass and noticed it."

Mac snorted. "Clearly Mr. Milsom needs a few lessons from Shani's prince."

"He's not mine, but you're right."

"She's a lot happier with that quarter-carat than you are with your wreath," Carly said quietly. "Give him credit for that, at least."

"I'll be real happy Saturday night," I told her. "You'll see."

I'm no dummy. That necklace was mine for one more day, and I was going to enjoy it just as much as if it really meant something.

DGeary   Want to hear the latest?
VTalbot   Bored to tears. Please.
DGeary   Hanna and the prince are engaged.

VTalbot Uh-huh. And I've got a tramp stamp to show you.

DGeary Serious as a heart attack. He gave her a $2M Harry Winston wreath.

DGeary Van? You there?

VTalbot When did you get so gullible? Stop wasting my time. Rory was going to ask her out. Poaching would be too challenging for him.

DGeary Truth. Dani saw them under the trees. Am forwarding pic to your phone.

⊚

VTalbot Status?

EOverton 45 confirmed.

VTalbot This is a joke.

EOverton Sorry, Van. Apparently Due is opening tomorrow night too.

VTalbot So???

EOverton I know Brett's going there.

VTalbot I don't care what he's doing. I want to know what you're doing to help me make this the event of the fall.

VTalbot It's Friday night and you're FAILING.

EOverton It's Friday night and maybe I have better things to do. Like go out.

VTalbot Don't make me laugh.

EOverton Maybe I'll go to Due if you feel that way.

VTalbot Maybe you should. Just don't ever expect another invite to anything from me. Including lunch.

EOverton You should be nicer to your friends.

VTalbot I am. I wish I could say you were one of them. But you obviously want me to fail.

EOverton You're doing that all by yourself.

⊚

HAVING THREE IN a room built for two has its problems. Closet space, for one. Privacy. Clashing taste in music. But what it's great for is ganging up on somebody who isn't spilling what's bugging her.

I turned on the lamp next to my bed a few minutes after Tobin called lights-out and I'd heard the clop of her sensible heels recede down the corridor. "All right, girlfriend," I said to Mac, "how about you tell us what's kept you so quiet all day?"

Mac rolled over to lie on her back while Carly and I propped ourselves up on our elbows like a pair of bookends. "It's nothing."

"Right," Carly said. "Nothing bugs me all the time. Keeps me from feeling good after my mani/pedi, and it's guaranteed to keep me quiet when I'm having dinner with my friends."

"Very funny."

"The operative word being *friends*," I said in a softer tone. "Talk to us."

Mac's chest rose and fell in a deep breath that could have been a sigh. "I'm terrified about testifying, that's all. Everyone staring at me. Having to see"—her voice hitched—"David again."

"He can't hurt you." Carly's tone was reassuring, but I'm not sure Mac believed her.

"Maybe not, but he can hurt my mum."

"How? He can't pack a pipe bomb into the courtroom." I'd never been in one, but even I knew that.

"Not that way. She'll see him and how he looks like my dad, and it will just be a mess."

"He looks like your dad?" Carly had seen Mac's half-brother the psycho a couple of times, but I never had. Not that I'm not happy about that.

Mac nodded, her head moving slowly on her pillow. "Same

eyes. Same jaw. He's the reason my parents divorced, you know. When mum found out, everything changed. Ended. Bang, it's over."

"Unlike my parents, who let it die a long, slow death," Carly said. "So slow I didn't even see it coming."

"When does your mom land?" I asked.

"The trial starts next Tuesday. She arrives Monday night. She's staying at the St. Francis."

"Are you staying with her?"

Mac shook her head. "No mercy from Curzon there. When I'm not in court, I'm supposed to be in class. As if anyone could concentrate on silly equations and essays while this is going on."

"That's pretty heartless," Carly agreed. "But at least you won't have to sit in the courtroom with him staring at you the whole time. My dad says they're keeping us in a separate room, and we go in by some other entrance than the one where the media are."

Mac looked at her. "So I can't sit with my mum?"

"I don't think so. But I bet they'd let her come in with us if you asked."

Mac smiled an evil smile. "I'd like to see them try to prevent it. She can play the Countess to the hilt when she wants to."

"Are we going to meet her?" I asked. "She sounds so scary, I wouldn't want to miss it."

"Mum isn't scary, she's lovely," Mac retorted. "And yes, of course you can meet her. She'll be coming up here to see me every day when we're not in court together."

"So let's see." Carly held up a hand and began counting off fingers. "We'll have a prince, a countess, and a princess-to-be right here at little old Spencer. All we need now is a—"

"Princess-to-be?" I broke in. "Who's that? Vanessa? Does she get to be *principessa* when her mom kicks off, or what?"

"Not her, silly," Mac said. "You."

I stared at both of them. "Oh, please." And flopped onto my back. "Puh-flipping-lease."

"I'm just sayin'," Carly added. "I hope you weren't planning to keep that necklace a secret, because it's all over school that he gave it to you."

"How do you know this stuff?" I demanded. "Do you pay people for phone tips, like the rags?"

"'Course not. I just listen, that's all. It's the rowing team that's Gossip Central. Those guys are worse than we are. Their girlfriends tell them everything, and they pretend they don't care and pass it on, and Brett tells me."

"What else are they saying? And if it's about my nonexistent sex life, I don't want to hear it."

Carly giggled and flopped back, too, so that all three of us admired the plaster medallions in the ceiling. "That's the stupidest rumor yet this term. No, you won't believe me."

"I'd believe you," Mac said. "If there's anything I've learned at this school, it's that the stranger it sounds, the more likely it is to be true."

"This is getting pretty strange."

"If you don't spill, I'll come over there and dump your bottle of water on you," I warned her.

"Rumor has it there's a new A-list in town."

"What?" Mac sounded confused, but I got it right away.

"I wondered when that would come out into the open."

"What do you mean?" Mac asked.

I opened my mouth, but Carly answered. "It's us," she said. "Haven't you noticed the signs?"

"Uh, no." Mac's tone was flavored with lemon. "I've been preoccupied with staying sane."

"You haven't noticed people saying hi to you in the halls that never noticed you before?" Carly asked. "People asking you what you're doing on the weekend, and then showing up at the same stuff? Vanessa giving up her table?"

"I noticed *that*," Mac said. "I also noticed she had it staked out the next couple of days with her minions, whom she then kicked out when her tier-one people arrived."

"Dani offered to lend me her iPod during free period so I could listen to the new Rihanna song," Carly said. "And rumor has it Emily and Vanessa are on the outs. Remember, the other day she tried to stay and sit with us? And Vanessa wouldn't let her?"

"Like we care," I scoffed. "Those people aren't friends. They're mutual back-scratchers. You guys are real, and Rashid is real. I have a feeling that us being friends with a prince is a big factor here."

"Not us," Mac said. "*You*. Who just happen to be friends with *us*. I'd love to know why he gave you that necklace. While we're sharing, why don't you share that?"

"Because he wanted to, I guess. He says it's like a thank-you for being his friend."

"That's some thank-you. It has to mean something," Carly said. "Is it like a really expensive promise ring?"

"*No*." This was beginning to scare me. "I already told you. The guy gives people presents. I made sure there were no strings attached, no promises, *nada*."

"Hm." Mac didn't sound convinced. "Maybe not out loud. But there's got to be something behind it. I think you should ask him."

"I did ask him. Maybe he does want more, but I told him I couldn't promise anything. Besides, I didn't want him to think I thought he had ulterior motives for giving me something," I said to the ceiling. "It'd make us both look cheap."

"Not for two mil," Carly said to no one in particular.

"I'm not his keeper. The man can do whatever he wants. If

he wants to make a pretty gesture and send our social status into orbit while he does it, that's fine with me." I got the conversation back on track. "You have to admit, it's interesting, this whole A-lister thing."

"Don't be smug," Mac said. "Even if it's true, who knows how long it will last?"

"Or even if we want it to." I shut off the lamp and snuggled under my duvet.

I might not be any kind of princess in the real world, necklace or no necklace. But it felt good to think I might be one in the social world of Spencer Academy, even if it only lasted a week.

Truth? After four years of being the loner with no friends, it felt pretty good.

chapter 14

POP! POP-POP-POPPITY-POP. A dozen flashbulbs went off in my face as I got out of the limo Manolos first, straightened, and took Rashid's arm. Half blinded, I put an arch in my spine and led with my hipbones as we walked the gauntlet of media and paparazzi toward the doors of Due. The dark raspberry silk of my vintage Lanvin whipped around my ankles, and I could practically feel the diamonds lying on my collarbones heating up with the intensity of the light.

"Whew!" Lissa said behind me. "This is good practice for the red carpet next month." She shook her hair, caught up into her mom's Art Deco diamond clip, back over her shoulders.

"And the courthouse next week," Carly added. "I counted three TV networks. It must be a slow night for news."

"I don't think it's us." Brett, who is half a foot taller than any of us girls, craned his neck over the crowd in the vestibule. "Panic! At the Disco is playing, but I don't think it's them, either." He looked again. "Oh. That explains it. My cousin is friends with Scarlett Johansson's agent. I just saw her duck into a private booth. She's filming here, and the rags are probably dogging her."

Whoever Brett's cousin had hired to plan the party for opening night, they were brilliant, as Mac would say. The place was done up in burgundy velvet and steel, with hardwood floors and an elevated balcony with a Plexiglas dance floor, packed to the edges with people and shimmering with lights. I might get away with dancing up there, with my long dress, but Lissa had better not try it. She wore a pale pink petal-hem baby-doll by Robin Brouillette, a San Francisco designer she'd just discovered who was a friend of Tori Wu—and anyone sitting at the tables under the elevated floor would be able to see, well, anything they wanted. The dance beats reverberated in my stomach, and I shrugged a little to the rhythm as Brett's cousin—Chase, his name was—materialized out of the crowd to show us to our booth.

"I've gotta see this." Brett, Gillian, and Rashid hung over the flat screen, which showed all of the little avatars we'd made this afternoon crowding into the booth. I'd made mine cute, a little brown anime figure with two ponytails and a two-piece suit (very mini, of course), with sky-high heels. Rashid's was tall and thin, with a poet shirt and a Heathcliff look. Funny how we see our inner selves, huh? Lissa had made a fairy wearing a bikini, Mac's was a glowery goth in a torn purple sundress, Gillian had uploaded the character she draws in art class, and Carly was a Regency lady with huge eyes and a tiara.

Brett's looked exactly like himself, which meant either he had no imagination or he was happy the way he was. I wasn't going to touch that one.

"Look, here's how you order drinks and food." Carly tapped a couple of icons on the screen. Ordering took a couple of seconds, and ten minutes later a girl in a black mini, white dress shirt, and tights appeared with the tray.

Panic! was scheduled to play later—their instruments already stood under the balcony—but I wanted to dance now, and the DJ was fine with me. I dragged Rashid out to a clear space under the hanging paintings and, okay, showed off a few of my moves. But even if he talks like he's fresh out of finishing school, he dances like he grew up around clubs. I tell you, we tore up that floor.

I don't even know when we got back to the table. It could have been hours or minutes, but whatever it was, our seats were taken. I skidded to a halt on the polished floor, dragging Rashid to a stop, too, like a big old boat anchor. I couldn't seem to get enough air into my lungs.

Lissa sat next to Kaz, looking like someone had lit her up from inside, yakking away at him. And beside Kaz sat Danyel, gazing at me over the rim of his tall glass of soda. Gazing through Rashid as if he wasn't even there.

I dropped Rashid's hand.

What were they doing here? Who had told them?

Danyel and Rashid couldn't be in the same place together. What was I going to do?

I fingered my necklace, tugging it away from my skin. *Breathe.*

Carly and Brett's chairs were empty. No help there. Mac looked from me to Rashid to Danyel and raised her eyebrows. No help there, either.

It was all on me.

"Surprise!" As I walked up to Danyel, he stood and hugged me. I detached Kaz from Lissa and hugged him, too. "How did you find us?" I sounded so chirpy and happy, as if my moment of panic had never happened. Go, me.

Kaz tilted his head toward Gillian. "She swore me to secrecy so we could surprise Lissa. It was too good to resist."

"Having fun?" Danyel smiled at me as if we were the only two people in the room.

"Yeah, this is great." I glanced over my shoulder at Rashid and stepped to the side to include him in the circle while I ran over what I remembered of the rules of introductions to royalty. Rule number one: the guy with the crown comes first. "Rashid, these are our friends from Santa Barbara, Danyel Johnstone and Kaz Griffin. They came to celebrate Lissa being a finalist for the Hearst medal. Guys, this is Prince Rashid al Amir. He's doing an exchange term at Spencer."

"Prince?" Danyel blinked and pulled in his chin as if he didn't believe me. "For real?"

"Yes, but please do not be uncomfortable." Rashid shook his hand, even though technically Danyel should have bowed or something. "We are all friends tonight."

Danyel looked at me, still a bit taken aback, and then his gaze dropped to my throat.

Blink.

Double-take.

Blink again.

"Are *those* real?" he blurted.

Much as I was tempted to make a joke about cubic zirconias, I couldn't very well do that with Rashid standing right there. "Of course. Pretty, huh?"

Then, before I could drag Rashid away, he spoke. "They were supposed to be a gift, but I am told they are merely to be a loan." He smiled at me. "And I must do as I am told."

"Wait. What? Whoa." Danyel, waved a hand, as if he were blind and feeling his way. "You mean you gave that to Shani?"

"I tried very hard to do so," Rashid said solemnly.

"Why?"

The very question the girls had asked me last night. But instead of answering, Rashid looked down his hawkish nose and straightened to military posture. "I was not aware that it was any business of yours." His tone would have chilled the drinks if they hadn't already been iced. Farrouk and Bashir, over in the shadows, straightened too. Farrouk slid one hand inside his jacket.

Great. All I had to do was introduce them, and already our fun night was teetering on the edge of ruin. "Come on, Rashid." I grabbed his hand. "Let's dance."

"We have just been dancing."

"And I want to do some more. Come on."

"No. Please sit down and tell me what right this person has to speak to you like that."

I forgot myself and rolled my eyes. "He's not a person, he's my friend. We're all friends here, like you said. Would you relax?"

Could this get any worse?

Yes, it could.

"You want to dance, Shani?" Danyel grabbed my hand and pulled me away from the group. "I'll dance with you."

Lord, help me now.

That wasn't a prayer. Honest. Even I knew better than that. But I was doomed if I went, and doomed if I didn't. At least this way, I'd get a dance out of the deal.

We made our way to the center of the dance floor, but instead of the funk and soul I wanted, the DJ segued into a slow blues number. I even recognized it. Stevie Ray Vaughan's "Riviera Paradise."

"So." Danyel took my hand and slipped one arm around my waist. "You the prince's girl now?"

I owed him an explanation. The time and the place stank, but hey, it had to be done. "I'm not anybody's girl."

"When a guy gives a girl this much bling, it usually means something, Shani."

"Like he said, it's just a loan. I'm giving it back to him tomorrow."

"But he wanted it to be for good, right?"

I shrugged. "Maybe. But what he wanted and reality are two different things."

"What I wanted and reality are, too, I guess."

Urgh. Poetic types. They talk in riddles and expect you to understand because your souls are knit together. I needed plain words. "What does that mean?"

"I thought we had something going."

"Maybe we do." I tried a smile, but he didn't smile back. Stevie's guitar wailed, content with the moonlight and the romance. Lucky him.

"Does he think the same?"

"We're just friends, Danyel. We've known each other since we were little kids." I flashed on a memory of Rashid and a dark room and how his kiss had made me feel—all hungry and shaky at the same time. Danyel and I hadn't done more than hold hands. What was my definition of *friends*? Was I so shallow that all I wanted was the kind with benefits?

"I thought you and I were friends. I thought we could be more than that."

"We can." I'd swear off the prince. Honest, I would. I had to sometime anyway, because by Christmas break, he'd have gone back to where he'd come from. I didn't want to be left with a bunch of busted possibilities where Danyel was concerned.

"How'm I going to believe that? You came to church with me last weekend, and this weekend you're freakin' it with him and wearing his presents."

His tone rubbed me the wrong way. "It's not like you put a sign on me saying Mine. And until you do, I can have friends."

"I can't afford to put diamonds on it."

Okay, a little jealousy was kind of sweet. But this sulky possessiveness when there was nothing but a "maybe" between us was getting old.

I pulled away. What a waste of a great slow-dance tune.

But he hung onto my hand and reeled me back in. "I'm sorry. I need you to listen for just one second, Shani."

"I'm listening." Back in his arms, I held myself a little aloof. Just sending a message that I was there under protest, you know?

"I want you to know I'm praying for you. Like, daily. Because you're my friend. And you mean a lot to me."

Now there was a contrast. One guy gave me diamonds. One guy prayed for me. Nine girls out of ten would have taken the first guy, hands down. But was I one of those nine girls, or was I the tenth who saw past the glam to the glow?

"I—I've been praying, too."

The corners of his mouth tilted up. "Yeah?"

"You and Lissa should engineer send and receive on your videos. Then you'd have heard me praying last Tuesday. First time."

"And what did you pray about?"

"Oh, just a general yell for help. I don't know if it worked or not, but it felt right."

"If it did, then it was." I snickered. "What?"

"When I saw you two facing off with each other a minute ago, I prayed. Sort of. But I'm sure the Big Guy had better things to do, because you saw how *that* worked out."

"I see that I'm the guy dancing with you. There's an answer to a prayer for you."

I had to laugh. "Okay for you. But here I am, stuck in the middle with not one, but two guys who've got a beef with me."

"Looks like you have to make a choice."

"Looks like."

He leaned in and pecked me on the cheek. A tingle ran down my neck and all the way to my hand. "May the best man win."

The song ended and when the DJ started sampling disco from the seventies, he took me back to our table, still smiling.

Rashid, however, was not smiling. He looked as though

someone had just crashed his favorite Hummer—and heads were going to roll.

Gulp.

Carly—oh, hey, she was back—bounced up. "I need to find the bathroom. Coming?"

Which, as you know, is code for *Danger! Clear the area.*

At this rate, my drink was going to be all ice water and no soda—and my dry mouth wasn't gonna get any of it. Still, I left it sitting there. When Carly's eyes start talking louder than the music, you'd better listen.

Safely in the ladies', we commandeered the handicapped stall together. "What's going on?"

While she did what she had to do, she gave me the sitch. "Rashid is furious that you did a slow one with Danyel. Is there more going on between you two than you told us?"

"Um. Maybe a little more. Maybe he kissed me."

"Kissed!" Carly's eyes widened as she finished up and did a hem check. "You never said you kissed the prince."

"Yeah, well, a girl likes to keep some things to herself."

"Well, a girl should think twice about it—Gillian would never have invited the guys up here if she'd known you two were serious. We thought you were crushing on Danyel."

"I was. I mean, I am."

"And you're kissing the prince."

Ouch. Don't look at me in that tone of voice.

I leaned against the stall door and rubbed a hand over my cheek, careful not to smear my sparkles. "I don't know what I'm doing. When I'm with Rashid, I kiss him. When I'm with Danyel, I *want* to kiss him. And now that they've found out about each other, neither of them wants to kiss me."

Carly gazed at me, obviously struggling between sympathy and *What were you thinking?* "Neither of them are the type to let the other be your beta boy," she said at last.

I nodded. "If I'd known it was going to get this whack, I'd have said no when Rashid asked if I remembered him that first day." With a deep breath, I changed the subject. "We'd better get back out there. Think Brett would dance with me?"

"No way. I don't want him getting shot by Farrouk."

Somehow this wasn't as funny as we both wanted it to be. We washed our hands and the music whumped us in the face when we opened the bathroom door.

So did Gillian and Lissa, practically running straight into us.

"Whoa, girlfriends!" I stopped Gillian from hitting the wall. "What's wrong?"

"That arrogant, selfish—" Gillian stopped herself from saying something she'd have to pray about, and tried again. "I'm sorry, Shani. I know he's your friend. But Rashid just left."

"Left?" I goggled at her. "What do you mean, left?"

"Just what I said."

Lissa chimed in. "He took the limo and Farrouk and Bashir and left us all stranded here downtown!"

And you know what? Instead of being angry or feeling abandoned or like I was going to lose him, a big happy wave inside me crested into a laugh. "Are Danyel and Kaz still here?"

"Are you kidding?" Lissa said. "They'd no more leave us down here alone than jump off the Golden Gate."

"Woohoo!" I pumped a fist at the ceiling. "It is time to par-tay."

"Are you crazy?" Carly's hands flew up helplessly. "You just offended Mr. Royalty and we're all probably going to get house arrest for the rest of term."

I grabbed her around the waist and waltzed her down the passage. "All the more reason to enjoy ourselves now. We've got the cutest guys in the room. We're dressed so fine we can hardly stand ourselves. And we're going to dance the heels right off our shoes."

And that's exactly what we did.

Until her watched peeped one o'clock and Gillian reminded Lissa that if she planned on a ten o'clock service in the morning, someone ought to find a cab. This wasn't as much of a killjoy as you'd think, because when everyone else loaded themselves into two of them, who was left over to drive back in Danyel's Jeep?

I think those girls engineered that on purpose.

Whatever—I wasn't complaining. Especially when he took my hand and held it all the way back to school. Rashid's hands were long and straight and fastidiously cared for. Danyel's were callused from picking guitar and waxing surfboards and holding summer jobs, his fingers sturdy and strong.

Was I making comparisons again? Was I finally going to make a decision? Because the time for that had come and gone. All I can tell you is that during the chaos of unloading three vehicles at the front steps of the school, Danyel stopped me from getting out. He leaned over and made as if to peck me on the cheek again.

Uh-uh. Decision time.

I surprised the you-know-what out of both of us by turning my head at the last second, so instead of my cheek, he got my lips.

My oh my, was it fine.

And then I did what I always do. I stepped back.

But this time I was laughing.

chapter 15

A New Princess for Yasir?

Spotted at the opening of Due, a new high-tech gallery
and restaurant in the Marina area of San Francisco,
was HRH Prince Rashid of Yasir with a bevy of beau-
ties in tow. But only one was wearing a custom-made
Harry Winston diamond necklace featuring the Star of
the Desert, a 30-carat yellow pear-shaped diamond.

And royal-watchers around the world know what
that means.

Yes, it seems Prince Rashid, young though he might
be, has made his choice of bride. But who is she?
Paris Match sent a special reporter to the West Coast
to find out.

Sources close to the prince at Spencer Academy,
a private high school for the scions of wealthy West
Coast families and the children of celebrities, say his
exchange term there has been a big success so far—especially when it comes to the social scene. With unlim-

ited access to money and the cachet of his royal status, the prince is a catch by any definition. But who is the mystery girl who has caught the royal eye?

Spencer student and fashion-scene regular Vanessa Talbot, daughter of the Principessa di Firenze and half royal herself, is in a particularly good position to comment. "I've known Shani Hanna since we were freshmen here together," said the brunette beauty, who was wearing a Prada leather skirt and a sheer blouse by Philip Lim 3.1 for the interview. "She's the nicest girl in the world—but I'd certainly never peg her as someone who would interest a prince. He has, after all, been hanging out with me and my friends almost exclusively since he arrived and we made him welcome."

So what is the mysterious Miss Hanna's appeal? While the school administration was tight-lipped on the matter, a student who did not wish to be named had her own take. "She's fun and nice and hangs out with the A-list. Why wouldn't he like her?" When questioned as to whom Spencer students considered the "A-list," the girl was quick to explain. "People like Lissa Mansfield, who's Gabe Mansfield's daughter, you know? His new movie is going to premiere next month and I'll probably be invited. And Gillian Chang, whose family owns the Formosa-Pacific Bank in New York. And Brett Loyola, whose family owns, well, big chunks of San Francisco. People like that." The girl paused to think a moment. "Not like Vanessa and Dani Lavigne and those people. Shani is too smart. She sees right through them."

While tinged with partiality and—may we say it?—a touch of jealousy, the unidentified student's comments are revealing. Because the next Princess of Yasir will need to be not only beautiful and socially expert, she'll need to be capable of inspiring love in not just one man, but an entire country. She'll also need to be connected.

Shani Hanna seems to be fulfilling that role instinctively. It remains to be seen whether the young woman, still only in her senior year of high school, will be the one who can tame the playboy prince and ascend the Lion Throne with him.

On location in San Francisco. —Roberta du Plessis, *Paris Match*

HALFWAY THROUGH MIDTERMS week, the only thing left to go was my art project. Since I was taking Jewelry Making, this was not as stressful as, well, Econ or Bio, but still. You try soldering a pendant with hands that don't shake just a little and see how far you get. On the whole, I was pretty happy with my project. I'd made several of the glass beads myself, which looked like little pearls with waves of color inside. The pendant was a composite Carly had done in Photoshop of all five of our faces, filtered as though we were looking through a rainy window. To finish, I had to attach it with a pair of silver chains and tie on the clasp. Once it was graded, I'd wear it with pride.

Unlike certain other necklaces I'd glommed recently.

It had now been a week and a half since the infamous Due opening, and the diamond necklace still sat in Ms. Curzon's safe. *But wait*, I can hear you thinking. *You were going to give that back to him the next day.*

I tried. But when I called him, it went straight to voice mail without even ringing. And then I had to hear from Vanessa Talbot, of all people, in our Macroeconomics class on Monday.

"How was the Due opening?" she asked me, leaning across the aisle like she never does.

"Fine. Great. SRO."

"We had a fabu time at Cream. Just a select few, and the celebrities, of course. I had such a hard time getting Channel Four to leave me alone. But a red carpet brings them in like flies, though I suppose you wouldn't know."

I could mention a few other things that attracted flies, too, but I didn't.

"Lucky Rashid." She sighed. "It must be nice, is all I can say."

In spite of myself, I had to ask. "What must be?"

She looked at me, surprised. "Didn't you hear? Spencer is sending a tutor to proctor his midterms. He flew home to Yasir for the week."

"Oh, that." I pretended this was old news. "I thought you meant something else. He told me he was going ages ago."

Not.

How was I supposed to return the necklace if the guy was out of the country? FedEx it to Yasir, care of the palace? Did FedEx even go to Yasir? Groaning inside, I tracked down Ms. Curzon and explained that the velvet box would have to stay where it was a little longer.

"That's not a problem, Miss Hanna," she assured me. "The prince will be back. He was called home unexpectedly for a short time, that's all. He is still expected to earn this term's credits at Spencer."

Which was sort of a relief. Because I didn't want him to jet out of my life thinking I was a two-timing skank. We'd been friends. Maybe a little more. He might not be part of my future anymore, but I wanted my present to be on good terms all the way around.

And that meant talking to him. Somehow. Sometime. Soon.

So, a week and a half later, I was getting antsy when I still hadn't heard from him. I'd heard from Danyel, though: Two prayer-circle videos, numerous phone calls, and a bunch of IMs. On Wednesday, an actual paper letter came, handwritten in a spiky scrawl.

> Dear Shani,
> Thought I'd go retro and send a letter. Hope you like my midterm English project.
> Yours, Danyel

Mine? I stared at the words. Somehow, knowing that his hand had held a fine-point blue Sharpie and guided these letters onto the paper meant more than a bunch of e-mail and instant messages. They seemed more solid, somehow. You couldn't just hit Delete and make them go away. You'd have to act—rip or burn or crumple—to negate the action that had made them.

Hmm. I'd obviously been spending too much time near the physics lab. Newton's Law, you know?

I opened the sheet folded inside the letter.

> To my lady, a sonnet
> I got no big house in Huntington Beach
> Got no connections to pick up and call
> No boss Ducati or Jaguar in reach
> No PDA to keep track of it all.
> What my God gave me is bigger than those
> I stand on the sand and check out the waves
> I talk straight up with the One that I chose
> And wish I could talk with the girl I crave.

If I owned this beach I still would want you
Having means sharing—hey, I can do that
When you drove away you took my heart too
Handle it lightly, 'cuz it's all I got.
I'ma wait here till you're ready to choose
Meantime a song's a good cure for the blues.
    —Danyel

I sat on my bed, shattered, and yet every atom of me glowing. How could I have spent even a minute thinking there was a choice between Rashid and Danyel? How could I have missed the totally obvious? What had I been thinking?

I scrabbled through my bag, through the stuff on my bed, tossed aside the books sitting on my desk. Augghhh! Where was my *phone?*

Then I spotted it on the carpet, halfway under the bed. I grabbed it with one hand and it went off like a fire alarm. With a shriek, I dropped it, then smacked my head on the bed rail trying to reach underneath and grab it before it went to voice mail.

Shani, you dummy, get a grip. It's probably not him anyway. "Hello?" I said breathlessly, pressing a hand to the sore spot on my skull.

"Hi, darling," my mother chirped.

"Mom!" I floundered through half a dozen things to say, then settled on a lame, "How are you?"

"*Superbe,*" she said in a flawless accent that told me she was either in Paris or had just been there. "I have a surprise for you."

With my mother, it's best not to guess. "Really? What?"

"Come downstairs and I'll show you."

I stalled. "Downstairs where? Where are you?"

"In a very nice room your headmistress calls the visitors' study. Daddy and I are waiting. Hurry, now!"

I FLEW INTO my dad's arms and squeezed him as hard as I could, breathing in the scent of Polo cologne and crushing the fine wool of his suit under my hands. "I'm so glad to see you," I said into his shirtfront. "What are you doing here?"

"Sharing our happiness with you." Smiling, Mom detached me and pulled me into a hug.

I recognized her dress from the Valentino show in Milan. "You look great. Love the color." The deep wine red showed off her coffee-colored skin, and she'd chosen a lipstick to match. "What do you mean, share your happiness? What's the good news?"

I gazed from one to the other as my dad ushered me over to the leather couch and waved me into it. Mom sat next to me while he took the chair kitty corner from it.

Mom smiled, the cat-got-the-cream one that meant she was pleased with something I'd done. But I hadn't done anything except pass my midterms (at least, I was pretty sure I'd passed with A's and B's) and make up my mind about a boy.

And neither of those options would make my parents leave Paris to come and see me.

It had to be something about them. "Don't tell me. Are you guys renewing your vows?" They looked at each other. Uh, okay. Guess this had never occurred to either of them. "You've bought another company?" Dad shook his head. "You're having another baby?"

"Good grief, Shani," my mother exploded. "Of course not!"

"Well, then? Tell me."

"I think you have something to tell us." When I just stared at her, Mom reached into her Chanel tote, its black patent as smooth as obsidian. She opened *Paris Match* to the centerfold and tossed it in my lap.

I stared at the photograph filling the upper half of the page. A guy and a girl sat in the grass under a tree. The girl was reaching out with both hands as a guy offered her a—

I blinked. That looked like—

It was. And the necklace was as clear as day.

I read the article so fast the type blurred. Then I got to the second picture. In it, Rashid and I were dancing, him behind me in some salsa hold with his hands around my hips. The light caught the necklace, bouncing off all those diamonds.

My eyes hurt. I lowered the magazine and closed it. "I don't get it."

Mom laughed. "I'd say you did. Where is that necklace now?"

"In Ms. Curzon's safe."

"That was sensible." My dad's baritone sounded solid, reassuring. Both of which I needed right now.

"You know this article is total speculation, right? Rashid and I aren't engaged. I'm only seventeen. That's crazy!"

"Age is irrelevant when it comes to the Kingdom of Yasir," my mother told me.

A needle of cold apprehension darted through my stomach. "What?"

She waved a hand at the paper. "You saw what it said. The Star of the Desert goes to the prince's future bride. It's been in the family for centuries. When Rashid's mother, Queen Zuleikha, got engaged to the Sheikh, the stone was set in a ring. Rashid had it reset as the centerpiece of that necklace."

And here I'd thought it was nice. Different. I didn't know the big old diamond had a *name*.

Never mind that. What was going on in my mother's perfectly coiffed head?

"It doesn't matter what it was, Mom. I'm giving it back to him. He's in Yasir this week, or I'd have given it back days ago."

"Given it back? Why?"

I stared at her. "Um, weren't you the one who sent me to those deportment classes where they tell you never to accept expensive gifts from men?"

"They weren't talking about princes, sweetie."

"The point is, we're just friends—in fact, at the moment I don't think we're even that. He found out I was seeing someone else and—"

"What?" Dad blurted.

I put up a placating hand. "Relax, Dad. He's really nice. I met him at Mansfields' this summer. His name is Danyel Johnstone and he's—"

"Wait, wait." Mom waved her hands, brushing the thought of Danyel out of the air. "What have you done?"

"Nothing." Identical scary faces. I swallowed. "I hope you can meet Danyel soon, that's all, because he's—"

"Are you telling us," my father said slowly, carefully, "that you're seeing some other boy? Not the prince?"

"Well, Rashid is out of town, so technically I—"

"Shani!"

Okay, this was getting weird. "What? Why are you looking at me like that?"

My mother took a calming breath. "You know it's unacceptable to be seeing this other boy while you're seeing the prince."

"Well, yeah, I get that, which is why I made up my mind, finally."

"And?"

I eyed him. "I don't get why it matters so much who I go out with. I haven't even seen you since—" Hm. How long had it been? "June."

"I care deeply when my daughter is involved with royalty."

"You don't have to worry about that anymore, then. Rashid got a little tweaked when Danyel showed up at this restaurant opening last weekend. That's when he took off and went back to Yasir."

"He'll be back tomorrow," Mom said.

I had like two seconds to wonder how she knew this, when Dad said, "You'll make it up with him. You'll tell this Danyel boy that you won't be seeing him anymore, and Rashid should be satisfied."

My jaw unhinged itself and hung open. "What?"

"You heard me, Shani. It's very important that your relationship with Rashid not be sidelined by irrelevant friendships."

Carly has this expression about stepping into an alternate universe, where people say things that make no sense and you wonder how you got there.

And how you're going to get out.

I was *so* in that place now.

Forming sentences was beyond me. So I went with small words. Simple and direct. "Why?"

He glanced at my mother. They came to some wordless agreement and my mom slid closer to me on the couch. She took my hand in both of hers.

Uh-oh. Something seriously big was going on. Because as you've probably figured out, my family isn't the most touchy-feely one you've ever met.

"Shani," she began, "remember when I told you that your great-grandmother married one of Rashid's great-uncles?"

For a second, I couldn't remember. Then a vague memory

came of wondering if we were fifth cousins twice removed. "Yes."

"Well, she wasn't the only one."

"Was he a bigamist or something?" I was trying to keep up, honest.

"No, no. I mean, that isn't the first time our two families have intermarried."

"I know." I tried to remember what Rashid had said. "Since, like, the sixteen hundreds or something."

"That's right. But what your mother is trying to say is that every three or four generations, our family—meaning my side— marries into Rashid's family." Dad looked at me as if this was supposed to mean something to me, but I must have looked as blank as I felt, because Mom picked up the story again.

"There are any number of brothers and sisters on both sides in recent times, so this is pretty easy."

"There are? How come I've never met any of them?" I wanted to know. "To hear you guys talk, you're onlies."

"We are, but our parents weren't," Dad said.

"So okay, but what does this have to do with me? Yeah, we've kind of bonded because he's some kind of cousin and we were friends when we were little. We appreciate each other for different reasons. But why does that mean I have to dump Danyel?"

"Because, sweetie—" Mom took my hand in a firmer grip. "—you're the fourth generation since your great-grandma."

I still didn't get it.

They gazed at me, waiting.

And then all the synapses in my brain lined up and fired at once. "You have *got* to be kidding."

Mom smiled with encouragement, as though she was telling me some huge secret. "Not at all, darling. We've known it for years. Why else would we make sure you had the best education money could buy? And deportment and elocution classes?"

"Uh, so I could run Dad's company someday?"

"No. You don't need to know the rules of precedence to run an oil company. We're very happy to hear that you're friends who appreciate each other—that's a wonderful place to start, now that you both are grown. Soon after you graduate, the Sheikh has given permission for you and Rashid to be married. You'll become Her Royal Highness, the Princess of Yasir. Isn't that exciting?"

CARLY TOLD ME later that she could hear me screaming from three floors away.

At that moment, every bad thought I'd ever buried, every lonely moment I'd ever had because my parents weren't there, every deserted Saturday afternoon of going to the movies with a maid came spewing out of me and into the faces of the two people who were supposed to love me.

Love me. Not sell me to the highest bidder.

"No!" I shrieked. "No way am I marrying him. And you can't force me into it!"

"No one is forcing you," my father tried to say, but I tromped right over him.

"This has all been a setup. That's why he's here, isn't it? It's not to take computer science classes, it's to romance me and make me fall for him."

"Well, of course we want you to be happy with your future husb—" my mother began.

"Don't say that word!" I threw my arms out and slapped a silk lampshade by accident. The lamp teetered dangerously before it rocked to a standstill. I grabbed a vase out of its niche in one of the floor-to-ceiling bookcases.

"Don't you dare!" Mom warned.

"Can you blame me?" I hefted it, calculating the distance past my father's ear to the fireplace behind him. "What else is in the plan? You gonna march me to the church the day after graduation?"

"No, of course not. Watch your language. You didn't grow up in the projects. And there'll be no talk of church. A state wedding would happen in Yasir, in the mosque."

"*Mosque?*"

"We've already talked to your headmistress about you dropping one of your electives and taking World Religions for the last two terms. You'll get private religious instruction, too, from an expert with the Yasiri embassy. No wedding will happen until you convert to the national religion, of course. The country wouldn't accept anything less."

I stared at them, my eyes practically standing out on stalks. "This can't be real."

My mother shook her head. "We converted several years ago, sweetie. It's not that big a deal."

"Oh, it's not," I said. "In that case, I think I'll be a Christian."

"You can believe what you like in private, but for all public occasions, you and Rashid must present a united front."

"Me and Rashid nothing," I managed to choke past the red gob of rage in my throat. "There is no me and Rashid. I'm not going along with any of this. You're crazy."

"Don't speak to your mother that way, young lady," my father said.

I laughed, a high hoot of disdain. "You have no right to tell me to do anything. You lost it when you checked me in here and left me behind for four years."

"You're our daughter," Mom said.

"No, I'm not. If I was, you wouldn't want to send me permanently to the other side of the world!"

Mom tried to put her arms around me, but I jerked away, still holding the vase. The smooth china felt slippery under my fingers. "I won't deny you were a surprise, but honey, the minute they put you in my arms I wanted you."

I faced her, my eyes filling with tears. I blinked them back. "Then how can you sell me off like this? Do you even know him?"

"Of course we do," my dad snapped. "Why do you think we've been spending so much time in the Middle East over the last five years? Rashid is a wonderful young man."

"How wonderful can he be if he's going along with this?"

"Shani, please—" Mom sounded as though she was going to cry.

That made two of us—and it still wouldn't match the tsunami of tears I'd cried since I was little, wondering why no one loved me and why my parents had more fun away from me than with me.

"I'm leaving. I have homework to do." With exaggerated care, I put the vase on a table next to the door and stalked out of the visitors' study.

Then I slammed the door as hard as I could.

Inside, over my mother's cry of distress, I heard the vase hit the floor and smash into a million pieces.

chapter 16

I BURST INTO OUR ROOM and Carly jerked her head out of the closet, where she'd been putting something away.

"Shani! What happened?"

I grabbed my purse and phone. "I'ma go away. Far as I can get." Tears ran down my cheeks and dripped off my chin.

Stupid tears. Wasted on those people.

"Shani, wait!"

Carly grabbed her own purse and a jacket and dogged me to the rain tunnel. Panting along behind me, she finally grabbed my hand and pulled me to a stop. "Will you tell me what's wrong?"

I shook my head and sniffled. She handed me a Kleenex.

I used it and kept going. "Gotta go."

Jogging beside me, she began to talk. And not to me. "Lord, this can't be good. Need some help here."

Okay, that got my attention. I pulled her through the glass doors of the field house and outside, where I hailed a cab. Once we were safely in the backseat, I told the cabbie, "Palace of Fine Arts." Then I turned to her.

Tears glimmered in her eyes.

For me.

My face crumpled again and I fell into her hug, sobbing like I'd never cried before in my life. Big, honking, hurtful sobs that lasted all the way down the hill. When I finally came up for air and had used every Kleenex she had, I felt hollow and empty.

All the rage had gone, leaving an acid trail of hurt. But I'd lived with that for a long time.

The cab dropped us at the Palace, but I turned my back on the depressing Rodin statues and headed for the misty coolness of the park instead. Up here on the hill, I could see the waves breaking on the shore below. The trees combed the fog with their branches, and it was quiet except for the *skreek* of the seagulls.

I could finally breathe.

And then I told Carly everything.

When I finished, I glanced sideways at her. Her face was so white in the pearly daylight that it was nearly green, and one last tear tracked its way down her cheek.

I'd used all her tissues.

"Here." With the cuff of my school blouse, I wiped the tear away. She shouldn't have to cry for me. I had enough tears for my own self.

"It can't be real," she said at last, like an instant replay of my own words. "They can't be serious. Who does that in 2009?"

"It is and they do," I replied somberly, and started on our second circuit of the park path. "But I don't care, I'm not going through with it. I've got nothing against Rashid. I like the guy, most of the time. But an arranged marriage? Are they insane?"

"It's one thing to find out you're a princess," she said, "you know, like in *The Princess Diaries*. But it's a whole other thing to have to marry a stranger to get there."

"And they completely threw up on the idea of Danyel. I'm not allowed to see him, just when I need him the most."

"If you're not going to marry the prince, I can't see that

stopping you. Why should it matter?" I blinked at her. Carly, giving the rebel yell? Whoa. "Don't give me that look," she went on. "There's a point in everyone's life when you have to stand up for who you are. If you're not going to be the Princess of Yasir, this would be that point."

"Girlfriend, you scare me."

She snorted. "A little scary isn't a bad thing. I learned that last term."

Memory seeped through the wall of my misery, and I connected the dots between her past and the present. "Wait a second. Didn't the trial start this week?"

She nodded. "I had to testify today. Mac is supposed to go tomorrow."

She hadn't been in the room when I burst in. "Where is she?"

"Her mom took her back to the St. Francis for dinner. She's a wreck."

"Mac or her mom?"

"Both of them, I guess. The countess—Margaret, her name is, but she asked me to call her Meg—had never seen David before he came into the courtroom. She didn't look so good when she came back into the judge's chambers to sit with us."

"I guess not." I tried to imagine it. "It'd be weird to see him, knowing your husband had cheated on you and he was the result."

"He didn't cheat on her, though. It all happened before they were married. He didn't know David existed until a few years ago. That's when he and Meg split up, and David started stalking Mac."

"Think Mac will last through the trial?"

Carly nodded, gazing out at the seagulls riding the updraft. "She's every bit as tough as she looks. She cares more about her mom's feelings than anything. It kills her that Meg won't forgive her dad."

"I'm not going to forgive *my* dad," I said grimly, returning to my own problems.

Carly turned to me, nibbling the inside of her lip. "I hope you do. Eventually."

"How can I?" I threw my hands in the air, and two gulls banked sideways, screeching in alarm. "They set me up in an arranged marriage! I'm not interested in making them feel all warm and fuzzy. I hope they—" I stopped myself from saying *shrivel up and die*. It would only upset her.

"I didn't mean for them," Carly said. "I meant for you."

"Huh?"

"Forgiveness. It's a two-way street, you know. They get forgiveness, you get peace."

"Believe me, I can get peace without that."

"You can try, I guess."

I turned on her. "You can't seriously think I'm going to forgive them for this. They can fly off into their self-centered sunset and never bother me again, as far as I'm concerned. They gave up their right to expect anything from me when they cooked up this stupid plan."

"Maybe so, but you're still responsible for what's inside you."

"You don't want to know what's inside me right now."

"That's why I'm praying, girlfriend."

Somehow this slapped me the wrong way. "Well, don't. I don't need anybody's help. I don't need people messing in my life. Not parents, not friends, not teachers, not anybody. Not even God. Where was He when the Sheikh was giving his high and holy permission, huh?"

"But Shani—"

I began to run.

"Shani!"

I dodged through the trees. The street was only a few feet away. I'd flag a cab and go . . . somewhere. The airport. I had all my credit cards in my bag. Maybe I'd catch a flight to Hawaii and spend a couple of days just lying on a beach until my brain fried and I forgot what my parents had done.

I wouldn't think about Mac and her problems. I wouldn't think about Carly and her unreasonable expectations. I'd just think about me.

It was all about me. And my survival.

Yeah.

Stupid tears, running down my face.

Stupid Carly, chasing me, shouting my name. Like I was going to stop.

Stupid blurry world and cars and—

I began to sob again, which was probably why I didn't hear or see the little silver Prius roll silently through the stop sign without even slowing down.

TEXT MESSAGE
To: PhoneList All
From: SysAdmin

Check out the article in this month's *Paris Match* (photo attached). And then check out Shani Hanna's baby bump. What will come first? Graduation announcements or birth announcements?

✉
To: DL_All_Students
From: NCurzon@spenceracad.edu
Date: October 21, 2009
Re: Text message

Please delete the defamatory text message on your cell phones that was sent out on the school phone alert system. Its speculations are, of course, completely false.

The Spencer phone and message server was hacked last night. The loophole in the OS that allowed this illegal entry has since been fixed. If any student has knowledge of who may have done this, please inform a faculty member immediately.

Thank you,
Natalie Curzon, M.Ed., Ph.D.
Principal

....

"DOCTOR VAN NESS to Emergency, please. Doctor Van Ness."

"I'm sorry, ma'am. Are you a member of the family?"

"I'm her mother. They told me she was in recovery. Is she all right? What happened? How badly is she hurt?"

"Let me page the doctor for you. Her sister is with her."

"Her *what?*"

"THAT GIRL HAS to leave. Both of you. Please. Nurse!"

"I am Lady Lindsay MacPhail of Strathcairn. Take your hand off my arm at once!"

"Please let us stay, Mrs. Hanna. We're her friends. We care about—"

"Out!"

WHEN I WOKE UP, the disembodied voices were a memory, the sounds rippling lazily like the long tails of ornamental goldfish. What time was it? What day was it?

Bright lights. Ow.

"Shani? Are you awake?"

A cool hand covered my forehead and I blinked my eyes open. "Mom."

She hitched a chair closer and stroked my cheek. "You had us pretty worried for a while there."

"Where am I?"

"SF General."

"What happened?"

"You tried to step on a Prius. It fought back."

I huffed out a breath in place of a laugh. Pain stabbed in—stomach, diaphragm, shoulders.

Guh. No more laughing.

"Your friend Carly said you ran in front of a car. According to her, you did a barrel roll over its hood and landed in the middle of the intersection. You hit your head pretty hard on the concrete. Fortunately the driver was a quick thinker. He jumped out and pulled you over to the sidewalk."

"Is she here?"

"The driver was a man, dear. No, he's not."

"Not him. Carly."

"She called 9-1-1 and the school, who called me. From what I gather, she rode in the ambulance with you."

Of course she had. What would I do without a friend like Carly? First Mac, now me. The sweet girl with the core of steel was making a career out of saving people's lives.

"She's not here now, though. I told them to go home."

"Mac was here, too?"

"I don't know. Who's Mac?"

"Redhead. Scottish. Attitude."

"Oh. Her. Yes, she was here this morning. But not for long."

"They're my friends. You shouldn't have chased them away."

Mom felt my forehead again, then adjusted the blankets over my chest. Just like a real mother. "I don't need your permission to decide what's best for you. What you need is to recover."

I didn't like the sound of that. How badly was I messed up? I wiggled my fingers. Check. IV in back of hand. Eww.

Eyes worked. Ears worked. Mouth obviously worked. I ran my tongue over my teeth. All there.

Toes? Check. Legs? Check. "What does the doctor say?"

"He says you're luckier than the Prius. That's going to be totaled."

Uh-oh. "I am okay, right?"

"For some reason, you didn't even break a toe. Your French tips are ruined, however, and you've got bruises everywhere. And he thinks you may have a bit of concussion, from the size of the lump on your head, so that's why they kept you overnight."

"I'm okay." Wow. Sweet relief spilled through me. "I'd hate to go to the premiere on crutches."

"That's the least of your worries."

"Why?" Was there some internal trauma no one had the guts to tell me about?

"I'm very sorry that the news about Rashid upset you so badly, darling. You shouldn't have run away. Then this would never have happened."

Oh, I get it. Being hit by a car was so my fault. Yep.

I turned my head, but there was nothing to look at except drawn curtains. I still couldn't tell if it was day or night. "I don't want to talk about it."

"We need to talk about it."

"Not now. I wanna sleep."

If my body couldn't escape the scheming harpy who had taken over my mother's body, my brain and the painkillers knew what to do. I slid gratefully into the dark.

. . . .

✉

To: vtalbot@spenceracad.edu
From: hrhr@gulftel.yz
Date: October 22, 2009
Re: Coming back

Thank you for your funny e-mail messages and Flickr photos. You are a true friend and I have appreciated every word. I was very sorry not to see you at the Due opening. I would have appreciated your support at what was a very difficult and disappointing time for me.

I have just arrived and am sending this from the limo. I look forward to seeing you again in Global Studies. Or perhaps sooner.

Rashid

. . . .

chapter 17

THE NEXT TIME I woke up, I came face to face with the biggest bouquet of flowers I'd ever seen outside of a hotel lobby. Birds of paradise, lilies, frangipani—it was like a chunk of some tropical island had landed on my bedside table.

> Dear Shani,
> I was devastated to hear of your accident
> and hope you are recovering quickly.
> Please accept these poor flowers and think
> of me each time you look at them.
> Yours,
> Rashid

I gazed at them with admiration, breathing in the fresh scent of greenery and the heady perfume of the flowers. Bashir had terrific taste. Or maybe he had a handbook of what flowers to send on every social occasion the prince would ever need. Because I wasn't fooling myself that Rashid had chosen them himself.

The handwriting on the card looked pretty authentic, though. Maybe I was dissing him. It wasn't his fault my parents—and maybe even his—had suckered him into a deal neither of us wanted. He was just as much a pawn as I, only he'd accepted his fate a lot more gracefully.

"Shani?"

Carly leaned in the doorway, followed immediately by Gillian, Lissa, and Mac.

I couldn't help the big, silly grin that spread all over my face like warm honey. "Girlfriends!"

They piled into the room as if it was our dorm, pulling up chairs, sitting on my bed, oohing over the flowers. Carly pulled an orange tiger lily out of the bouquet, snapped off most of its stem, and tucked it behind my ear.

"There," she said with satisfaction. "Good accessories can overcome even blah hospital gowns."

I pulled her into a hug. "The only accessory I need is you guys. Thanks for saving my life, by the way."

"You'd do the same for me." She made herself comfortable on the edge of the bed.

"She hasn't had as much practice as you," Mac told her.

Then I looked more closely at the two of them. "What's with the suits? Is that more Chanel?"

"Vintage sixties." Mac plucked at the navy-blue boxy jacket with its signature cream piping. "Mummy dug it up and brought it with her for the court case, since this isn't my usual thing. She thought it would be more appropriate."

I glanced at her feet, where she was styling her Louboutin ankle boots. "That's better. You had me worried for a minute. So you guys had to appear again today?" I thought for a second. "What is today?"

"Thursday. You stepped on that Prius yesterday," Carly said. "And yeah, we did. Today David's lawyer cross-examined us."

"I bet that was fun," Gillian said. "Did you wipe the floor with him?"

"Mac did." Carly smiled at her. "But we didn't come all the way over here to talk about that." She patted my hand—the one without the IV. "We want to know how you are and when you're coming back."

I glanced at the door, as if a doctor would come in and tell me. "I don't know. I'm sore, and I banged my head, but nothing big."

"Thank You, Lord," Lissa told the ceiling.

"I'd go back today, if I could."

"Rashid's back at school," Gillian said.

"On second thought, I think I'll finish out the term right here." I pulled the sheet out from under Carly and hauled it up to my chin.

"Are those from him?" Lissa waved a hand at the flowers.

"They're probably from Bashir, but Rashid signed the card."

"Oh, man." Gillian looked pained. "*We* should have sent flowers."

"Trust me, I'd rather look at his flowers and see you," I assured her, "not the other way around."

"Carly said something bad happened when your parents came to see you yesterday at school," Lissa said a little hesitantly, "but she's being such a clam we couldn't get it out of her."

"You didn't say I could tell." Carly made a sorry face. "And with your mom kicking us out this morning and court today it didn't come up again."

"No big." I looked at them, one after another. "My parents only flew halfway around the world to flash me the big headline that—"

"Shani!" My father walked in, stepping all over my words, my doctor trailing behind him the way Bashir and Farrouk trailed in Rashid's wake. "I'm so glad to see you awake and feeling well enough to have visitors."

Yeah, I bet. "Girls, this is my father, Roger Hanna. Dad, these are my roommates, Carly and Mac, and our friends, Gillian and Lissa."

Dad nodded at them. "Nice to meet you girls."

"Carly is the one who saved my life."

"So I understand. Also the one who masqueraded as your sister."

She and I exchanged a smile. "I so see the family resemblance," I said. "You have my grandma's eyes."

"I don't think telling those kinds of lies is so funny." Sheesh, had he left his sense of humor on the luggage carousel at SFO or what?

"There are other kinds that aren't so funny, either," I said pleasantly.

The doctor, who had been checking numbers on the machines ranged on one side of the bed, cleared his throat. Carly grabbed the moment and slid off the bed. "It was great to see you, Shani. We'll be going now."

"'Bye, guys." I felt as pathetic as I sounded as all the people I really wanted around me trooped out of the room, glancing at my father as they went. When I couldn't hear their voices anymore, I sighed.

Now I really felt sick.

The doctor typed something on the wall-mounted keyboard. "Your vitals are good, Shani, and we'll do a couple of checks on your responses to make sure, but I think I can release you tonight."

"Yeah?"

"Just promise me you'll lie low for a couple of days. No late-night partying, no alcohol, no sports until after the weekend."

"No problem." What, did the guy think I'd been drinking when I'd run out into the intersection? With another sigh, I let it go.

"I'll give you some time to visit with your dad while I do the paperwork, and then he can take you back to school."

Oh, joy. Could we skip Part A and go straight to Part B?

Guess not.

Dad reached over and plucked the flower out of my hair. He looked around for somewhere to put it, and finally settled for tucking it in at the bottom of the bouquet, where it hung suspended, just out of reach of the water.

"What did you do that for? I liked it."

"It's not respectful of Rashid's gift."

"I wore his diamonds. Why not his flowers?"

He looked at me as though he wanted to call the doctor back and tell him to rethink my release. "Is this a side-effect of painkillers, Shani? All this crankiness?"

"It's a side-effect of *you*, Dad. You come in here, chase my friends away, take away my flower, and then criticize me."

He gave me a long look, but there was no anger in it. I was almost sorry. If I couldn't get love out of him, then at least we could pick a fight. "I'm going to cut you some slack, because you've been through an ordeal. But before they release you and we go back to Spencer, we need to talk."

The sleep strategy probably wouldn't work, and he sat between me and the door. "Dad, you want one thing. I want something completely different. End of talk."

"I think if you knew the circumstances, you might reconsider your position."

"I doubt it."

He gazed at me from the chair, frowning. "When did you get to be so . . . obdurate?"

"Oh . . . somewhere between being shipped off to boarding school and sold to the highest bidder, I guess."

"Your mother and I love you, Shani. We want the very best for you, which is why we've spent so much time making sure you had the best education money could buy, that you connected with people who could help you in your adult life, that you had mentors and caretakers with international interest."

"You make me sound like those pandas in China."

He ignored me. "This arrangement between our family and the Sheikh's is the best thing that could happen to any young woman."

"You should go find one who appreciates that, then."

"I believe you'll come to appreciate it once you know the truth. You said something yesterday, when we saw you at Spencer, about running PetroNova some day."

I nodded. Though at this point, no matter how much education I had, being hired by my father as anything more than a mailroom clerk seemed pretty remote.

"Well, the truth is, without you there *is* no PetroNova."

Or maybe not. "What do you mean? Can I work there after I graduate from college? Because, Dad, I totally plan to apply to Harvard Business School and Stanford. I just have to decide if an M.B.A. or a doctorate in organizational studies would be a better—"

He shook his head. "No, no. That's not what I meant." He fell silent a moment, as if he were organizing his arguments. Then he looked up. "Nearly twenty years ago, when I was fresh out of college, I spent a winter in Yasir with my grandmother and her husband."

Okay, I didn't get the connection, but I'd play along. "Rashid's grand-uncle or whatever."

"Right. I was like you are now, burning with ambition. I had big plans to do graduate work in petroleum technology, thinking I'd focus on abandoned wells and recovery."

"So what happened?"

"I'd met your mother in my junior year, and we had plans to marry the summer after graduation. I was twenty grand in debt from student loans, and looking at more. I'd always known our families were tight, but I didn't know how tight until the Sheikh, who was a young man then, made me an offer I couldn't refuse."

"What was that?"

"In return for a continuing alliance between our families, as had been going on for generations, he would finance a forty percent stake in a petroleum exploration company. I'd run it, he'd act as a partner until it was off the ground, and we'd begin by drilling in some of the more remote parts of Yasir."

Fragments of conversations I'd heard when I was a kid flickered in the back of my memory.

"That was that big well that came in in the nineties, wasn't it? The one that saved the first President Bush's butt during whatever war that was?"

My father nodded. "Sales of petroleum from Yasir made it, um, economically feasible for the U.S. to bring certain parts of its strategy in the Middle East to a swift close."

"But, Dad, I still don't get what this has to do with Rashid and me."

"I told you, honey. I promised an alliance. Our family bloodline includes a prophet that validates the royal family's claim to the throne. The continuation of the line means the House of al-Aarez stays, in their minds, blessed. And that means you and Rashid."

"But how can you make that promise when I wasn't even born? And I've gone my whole life not knowing anything about it. Did Rashid know?"

"He has always known he would marry for the good of his family. And you have to admit, prophets aside, the oil in Yasir has been very, very good for the house of al-Aaraz."

"And for the house of Hanna." I couldn't keep the bitterness out of my tone. "But this doesn't change anything, Dad. I'm still not going to marry him. I'm going to graduate from Spencer, go to college, and have a career like a normal person."

"Then all of us will have to face the consequences. Because normal isn't for people like us."

"What consequences? You say to the Sheikh, 'Hey, she didn't go for it. Let's find another cousin for Rashid.'"

"There aren't any cousins who have been brought up to this job the way you have. Everything you are, all the experiences you've had, have been tailored to make you the perfect Princess of Yasir."

Of all the things he'd said to me, that flat-out scared me the most. Cold crept over my skin. "I'm not any princess, or anybody's version of what a princess should be. I'm me. Shani. I'm my own self and I'm going to stay that way."

"If you do, you'll put us all at risk."

"For what? Is Yasir going to declare war on the U.S. because of me?"

"Of course not. But I'll tell you what the Sheikh will do. He'll pull his forty percent stake. And PetroNova will fail. Your mother and I will lose the house in Lake Forest. We'll lose the corporate jet and none of us will be able to travel again, including the cruise down the Loire and the shopping trip in Paris we promised you for graduation. And it won't stop there." He leaned in toward me. "You'll be pulled out of this school and sent to public school in Chicago for the rest of your senior year. You'd better forget about Harvard Business School or any other college, because there won't be any money to send you. And it goes without saying that all your credit cards will be cancelled. You'll be lucky to keep whatever's in your savings account. Because, honey, there's no trust fund."

I sat there in my cheap cotton hospital gown and stared at him. "Are you kidding me?"

"I have never been more serious about anything," my father said. "If you don't accept that necklace he gave you and announce your engagement to Rashid, our life as we know it will be over, and our family will be completely ruined."

chapter 18

I HAD STREP in my freshman year, so I knew that Ms. Vallejo, one of the biology teachers, was also Dr. Vallejo, in-house doc. She must have been in her thirties, but sporting jeans and a plain white T-shirt under her blue school blazer, she looked about twenty-five.

"You have two choices," she said, sitting on the edge of the exam table while I kicked back in one of the chairs. "You can stay in your dorm room for the weekend and flog your roomies into giving you the peace and quiet you need to recover, or you can stay here in the medical suite, which is off limits to everyone except me, Ms. Curzon, and family members."

Family members? Well, that was a no-brainer.

The Media Communications students jacked my laptop into the comm system and I took my Friday morning core and Life Sciences classes (except Phys.Ed.) in our dorm room by video link. I'm not a geek like Gillian, but I do love the perks of technology.

Carly brought my lunch on a tray, along with a plate for herself. Barbecued ribs and poached kale, which I could sort of fool myself into thinking were collard greens. And, of all things, sweet potato pie. Bless Dining Services. If anyone was jonesing for comfort food right now, it was me.

"So Brett wants to know if we want to go up to Napa this weekend, now that midterms are over." Carly licked sauce off her fingers. "They're harvesting the grapes. His parents are going up and there'll be a big cookout and free concerts in town."

"Oh, man. That sounds great."

She pointed a rib at me. "No dancing for you. You're to sit on the veranda in the shade and have people bring you cold drinks."

"You know I can't go. The doc will have a fit."

"Would you rather sit in this room by yourself all weekend? At least in Napa you'll have us, and Brett's mom can't wait to get her hands on you. She says don't worry about a thing."

I gazed at her, puzzled. "Why would she care? And how does she even know?"

"I hope you don't mind. I told the girls the deal with you and Rashid, and Brett, too. When he told his mom, she freaked. I think she's behind this whole thing."

"A mom plot to get me away from my parents and Rashid?" Wow. I didn't care who Carly told. But I could hardly believe that a woman I hardly knew would care two cents about what happened to me.

"Where are they, anyway?" Carly asked.

"My parents? At the Four Seasons. They're not leaving town until they get the answer they want."

Carly's eyes widened and she looked a little scared. I filled her in on what my father had unloaded on me last night. Halfway through, her mouth dropped open in shock, and stayed that way until I was done.

"I can't believe it," she said. "I can't believe they'd treat you like that. You're their *daughter*, not a stock portfolio."

I shrugged, and then regretted it. "Ow. Not much I won't

believe anymore. Back to the fun part. I don't think I'll make it to Napa without drugs."

"You have plenty of those." She glanced at the miniature pharmacy on the desk next to me. "So let me get this straight. Your folks aren't leaving until you say yes to Rashid, even though you're only seventeen. If you don't, you get disinherited, and they lose their company?"

Disinherited. Trust her to sound so very Austenese. "Pretty much."

Her eyes narrowed. "I don't care if we have to clunk you on the head with Gillian's physics book to knock you out. You're coming to Napa and getting away from those people."

I tried to laugh, but it came out more of a cautious sigh. "Ma'am, yes, ma'am."

To: Dijon@mac.com
From: CAragon@spenceracad.edu
Date: October 23, 2009
Re: Napa

Hi, Danyel. I know this is late notice, so I hope you get this in time. Shani was in a car accident on Wednesday. She's OK, but the girls and I want to take her away from here for some R&R. She's having major parent issues and needs to be with us for a couple of days.

If you can come, call me at 408-555-1002. I'm attaching a map of how to get to Brett's parents' vineyard in Napa. That's where we'll be. I hope we'll see you.

Our girl needs you.

Carly

It took me half an hour of—as Mac said—"creaking 'round the room like a crone" to get a bag packed, but at least Mac carried it downstairs for me. Two hours later we were all in Napa, breathing in the sweet smell of freedom and ripening grapes as we climbed out of the limo.

"I've been a lot of places," I said, walking to the terrace rail and looking out at the hillside and its terraces of vines, "but this is one of the most beautiful, ever."

"*Grazie.*" I turned to see Mrs. Loyola, whom I hadn't laid eyes on since we stayed at their house last spring. "I hope it helps us help you recover, Shani."

I stiffened in both surprise and pain as she gave me a soft, gentle hug. Then she held me away from her. "You poor child," she said. "Forgive me for prying the whole story out of Carly. I can't make up for this in any way, but maybe we can get you well enough to face it, at least."

Whoa. How come Brett got such a great mother, and I got the scheming harpy?

At the vineyard, the Loyolas ate on Italian time, which meant anytime after eight. So while the sun slid languidly over the shoulders of the hills, Brett and Mac took off to show Carly how to ride a dirt bike. That girl is courage on feet. I can do a lot of stuff, but I like solid metal around me when I'm zooming around in top gear.

I lay on a nice squashy chaise longue on the veranda, over-looking the hillside heavy with grapes, and listening to birds and the sound of a fountain somewhere out of sight.

Bliss.

The only thing that would make it perfect would be—

"Something to drink?" Mrs. Loyola put down a tray with a

pitcher of iced tea and a couple of glasses on the glass table next to me.

"You're a mind reader."

"No, only selfish. I wanted some, myself. I'm only sharing it with you so I won't look bad."

This time I could laugh without pain, or maybe it was all the pills I'd taken so I could survive the ride up here. Didn't matter. It felt good to laugh.

"Where did Lissa and Gillian go?"

"They dragged Jeremy and that other boy—Jake?"

"Tate."

"Right. They went off into the grapes to have a look. Gillian's never seen live grapes in the wild, as it were. I think she wanted to capture a bunch and bring them back to eat. Though that'll probably be a surprise. Cabernet grapes aren't exactly Thompson seedless."

"Do we get to stomp them?"

She laughed and shook her head. "No stomping here. It is harvest, though. The vineyard workers go down the rows with the tractor"—she pointed into the distance—"and load the grapes into half-ton plastic bins. Those go on a flatbed truck, which takes them to the winery."

"Aren't you a winery?"

"Afraid not. We're what they call a boutique vineyard, only fifteen acres. We supply one of the bigger ones. It's a hobby for my husband and an excuse to get out of the city for me."

"I hear you," I said, a little too fervently.

Her eyes were so kind. "I hope I didn't say anything I shouldn't have when you arrived. The situation upsets me. I apologize if I let my feelings go and embarrassed you."

"Don't." I wished I had the guts to touch her hand. "The situation upsets me, too. Which is way understating it."

"I wish I could do something. All I can do is pray, though, so I've been doing that."

I blinked. "Pray?"

"Yes. You've heard of it?"

With a roll of the eyes, I said, "I'm surrounded by praying friends. I'd have to be deaf not to hear of it."

"You don't know how lucky you are," she said softly.

"Lucky? My parents are selling me to a prince for a forty percent stake!"

"Not about that. To have friends who care so deeply. Who go to the Lord for you. That's a huge gift."

"I know it." I did. I just didn't know what to do with it. Maybe, with the situation the way it was, I should start looking into that.

"I can't tell you how thankful I am for your friend Carly," she went on. "Since he started going with her, Brett is a different person. I don't get calls in the middle of the night from our restaurant managers, telling me he's wandering on the waterfront with his friends, stoned out of his mind. I don't hear from the police anymore. He studies, he rows . . . he actually made the dean's list for the first time, did you know?"

I shook my head.

"Carly is so fearless about being who she is in her faith that it shook him up. It made him see me differently. He actually *talks* to me."

To hear her tell it, this was the equivalent of getting a two-million-dollar necklace. But she probably already had one of those. So it was even better.

"So that's why I browbeat you all into coming this weekend. To thank you for being his friends."

Or for being Carly's friends. But . . . wow. What was going on with Brett, anyway? He couldn't be putting it on, because Carly would see right through that. And if she didn't, Lissa would. Could it be possible that Gillian was right? That God worked through people and changed them, and then started changing everything around them?

Was I sitting here listening to this sweetheart of a lady, who had tears in her eyes, she was so happy, because one day in junior year, Carly had decided that she needed God?

Did it really happen like that? Could it happen to me?

Because it was becoming plain that I wasn't doing a very good job of managing my own self. Even my ability to trust myself was kind of shaky. Here I was, looking at the powers my girlfriends seemed to have because of this God thing—and I had nothing.

Why did God keep sending me praying people?

What was He up to?

If I was quiet during dinner (something Mr. Loyola called "meat gravy" that was more like this massive stew and tasted amazing), they must have chalked it up to the drugs, because no one bugged me about it. And when I went upstairs early, no one said anything then, either.

Except before I went, I found Mrs. Loyola in the kitchen.

"Um, Mrs. L.?" Instead of answering, she turned and gave me a hug. "Do you have an extra Bible lying around?"

No fuss, no muss. She just took me into a room full of books and fabric and big, clumsy pencil sketches tacked on easels, and dug one out from under a pile. "Keep it."

I brushed off the pebbly leather binding. "I can't do that."

"Sure, you can. I have a couple of different versions for studying. This is the NIV. It's pretty easy to follow."

"But I—"

"Shani." She stopped me with a look. "Let me do this one thing for you."

One thing? Out of the dozens she'd done for me today alone? "I, um . . . okay."

She was so practical about it, as if I'd asked for a hot water bottle or another pillow. I took the Bible back to my room, brushed my teeth, climbed into bed, and looked at it.

My grandmother used to read me passages when I was a kid, and she'd quote stuff like, "Train a child in the way he should go, and when he is old he will not turn from it." That was a favorite when I'd been bad. But there were interesting stories, too. The lady who freaked when she found one of her gold coins was missing, and tore her house apart until she found it. The guy who bought up some real estate because he'd heard there was a treasure buried there.

But I didn't know what I was looking for. And if I did, I didn't know how to find it. But there had to be a reason why my friends went to this book when they were down about something, or when they needed to make a decision.

Um, Lord? You there? I could really use a hand, here. I opened it on a random page.

"For God said, 'Honor your father and mother' and 'Anyone who curses his father or mother must be put to death.'"

Oh, gack. Thanks a lot. I nearly gave up then and there. But when I closed it and looked out the window, there were all those rows and rows of grapes in the moonlight. Gillian told me once that people produced fruit, too. Like honesty when you talk. And kindness, like Mrs. Loyola. And love and joy.

Hm. Maybe there was a reason Jesus was always talking about vineyards. I flipped to a different place, looking for stuff about fruit. At the very beginning of Proverbs it said:

"... they will eat the fruit of their ways
and be filled with the fruit of their schemes.
For the waywardness of the simple will kill them,
and the complacency of fools will destroy them;

but whoever listens to me will live in safety
and be at ease, without fear of harm."

Okay, I could live with that. Because my parents were welcome to the fruit of their schemes—it wasn't going to be me eating it, that was for sure. Proverbs was interesting. I kept going.

"Choose my instruction instead of silver,
knowledge rather than choice gold,
for wisdom is more precious than rubies,
and nothing you desire can compare with her."

Hah! Rubies or not, if that wasn't referring to a certain necklace I could name, I didn't know what was. I liked what it said about choosing. Because as far as my dad was concerned, I had two choices: marry Rashid or face total ruin. There was no Plan C.

But what if there was? "Choose my instruction," it said right there in black and white. What did it mean to be instructed by God? Was He like Mr. Milsom in the bio lab, ranting at people about cleaning up their benches? No, probably not. It probably meant just what I was doing. Reading. And listening.

Okay, Lord, I don't know anything about this, but I am for sure listening now. Can You give me some instruction, please? Do I really have the power of choice here? Or are You gonna make me obey my mother and father so they can hand me a big helping of the fruit of their schemes? Is that what You want for me, Lord? Because if it is, I'm not liking it much.

I know I don't have any right to come around asking, but can You help me choose a path? Show me what I'm supposed to do? Because I don't have anywhere else to go. You're it, big guy.

And one of us has to do something. Soon.

chapter 19

I HOBBLED INTO THE dining room the next morning to see Danyel Johnstone sitting at the table, yakking it up with my friends as if he'd been here all along.

My mouth opened, but no sound came out.

"Hey, Shani." He got up and came around the table to give me a hug. *Ow.* "I got in at two in the morning. I didn't think you'd appreciate me waking you up to say hey."

"How . . . what . . ."

Carly put up her hand as if she were swearing to tell the truth, the whole truth, and nothing but the truth. Which I suppose she's had a lot of practice at lately. "I did it. I sent him an e-mail yesterday with a map telling him how to get here. If you're going to kill me, do it in private, okay?"

"Kill you?" Finally, brain caught up with mouth and produced words. "I don't think so."

I glanced up as Mrs. Loyola came through the door to the kitchen with a big plate of French toast—a refill, obviously. The hoglips around the table had apparently not waited for every last one of us to haul our butts out of bed. "Morning, Mrs. L."

"Hi, Shani. I'm so glad you invited Danyel."

"Do you really have rooms for all of us?"

"I have him in the sunroom on the daybed. It'll be fine to sleep in, but it gets warm in the afternoons."

"You can put me on the floor if you want," Danyel said. "Like I said last night, I don't care."

"The next person who turns up gets the floor." She filled a pitcher of syrup and put it on the table. "*La Gallina Contento* is officially full. The last time that happened, I had the entire rowing team here for the weekend. The grocery store in town probably hasn't recovered yet."

She raised an eyebrow at Brett, who shrugged. "What can I say? We eat a lot."

After breakfast, Lissa and Gillian made Tate wash the dishes while they dried. Carly and Brett made like vapor and vanished, and I found myself walking (slowly) across the lawn with Danyel.

I think the whole maneuver was planned. Those girls are good.

"So, car accident." Danyel stretched out on the grass, which sloped to a stand of oaks and then the grapevines beyond. In the distance, the tractor *put-putt*ed in slow motion down the rows. "Feel like telling me what happened?"

"You mean Carly hasn't already?"

"She gave me the headlines. I'm having a hard time believing them. It's like reading *News of the World* if you're not one of the Men in Black."

So I filled him in. It took a long time—not including the parts where he got up, stalked around the lawn saying not very nice things, and then sitting down again to get the next installment.

"I gotta tell you, I'm having a real hard time with this." He folded himself up beside me as if he intended to stay put this time. "I don't know how you handle it."

"I'm not," I confessed. "Mostly I'm just whining to my friends and crying. I finally tried to read some in the Bible last night."

His warm brown gaze felt as good as sunshine. Better. It went all the way through me. "Yeah? Did it help?"

"I don't know." Then I reconsidered. "Yeah, it did. My dad says I have two options. But the place where I was reading showed me I might have another one. It said to choose instruction over riches."

"So, what—you're going to go to college instead of get married?"

"Duh. I don't think that was the instruction it was talking about. That's, like, reading the Bible, right? And listening to God."

His gaze never left my face. A quality I discovered I liked in a guy. Not that there was much I didn't like about Danyel.

"You surprise me," he said.

"Why? Did I read it wrong?"

"Not that I can tell. The Spirit must be working it with you."

My whole body just . . . suffused. I felt warm all over, right to the heart. But was it because I had Danyel's complete attention, or his approval, or because I was happy about the Spirit doing its thing?

Oh, stop analyzing it and just be happy you can feel anything at all. Think about this time last year, when you were walking around the halls at school like a robot, with nothing to look forward to but graduation. No friends, no life, no joy about anything except seeing how far you could run up your credit cards before your dad called to yell and give you some attention.

"This situation stinks," I said, "but I guess I can be happy about that. The Spirit, I mean."

"You guess? I know I'm happy about it."

"But I'm not like you. You and Lissa and Gillian and

Carly . . . you're all God's little BFFs. I don't have any clue what I'm doing."

"You're going to the Bible for answers, aren't you? That's what us BFFs do."

Huh. Maybe. "I'm going to you, too."

"Another thing BFFs are for. God wants us to find the answers. And to give us more questions to ask Him and each other."

"You being here is an answer. And I didn't even pray . . . for that." A lump formed in my throat and I swallowed it down.

He smiled at me. "I bet Carly did."

Then, Carly-like, she acted. And it was totally the right thing to do.

"So if you read, and you prayed, and it looks like the answer is clear, what are you going to do about it?" he asked.

"I know what I want to do. Ask some more questions. Go to college. Get that M.B.A. But that still doesn't tell me what to do about my dad and PetroNova and everything else."

He picked a blade of grass out of the lawn and began folding it up into sections, like an accordion. "You said he chose to do that, right? Make the deal with the Sheikh even though he wasn't the guy who would have to keep it?"

"Yeah."

"So you didn't make any deal, from what I can tell. They can't force you."

"Maybe they can. Maybe they can throw a bag over my head and fly me to Yasir and make me marry Rashid."

"I think there are laws against that."

"The Sheikh *is* the law there."

"I don't think you have to worry. I didn't have much time to get to know Rashid, but he didn't seem like the kind of guy who'd want his fiancée treated that way."

"That's the thing." I wrapped my arms around my knees. "He *is* a nice guy. For a while there, I liked him a lot."

"More than me?" He grinned like it was a joke, but I shook my head.

"He did it for me physically, but it was always you who could do it for me all the other ways."

"Whoa." He blinked, fast, the way people do when firecrackers go off under their noses. "You got physical with that guy?"

"Would you relax? We just kissed."

"Kissing leads to other stuff."

I rolled my eyes. "You sound like my mother. And if it were any of your nevermind, I'd tell you it didn't lead to anything. Nothing. *Nada*. Got it?"

"Got it."

"Besides, I kissed you."

"That was an accident."

"Thanks a lot."

"Stop it, girl. When we get around to kissing for real, it won't be an accident."

"Promises, promises."

He grinned at me. "I always keep 'em. Consider yourself warned."

Shivery anticipation tingled all the way down to my feet. I hoped it wasn't visible. "So, getting back on topic," I said, "is that what you think I should do? Tell my dad I can't keep a promise he made before I was born? Let him lose his company, our house, the whole enchilada? That seems really harsh."

"Maybe, but when people gamble, sometimes they lose. And what if God has a plan for your life that doesn't include being Princess of Yasir?"

"Seems like He does, huh."

"I'd say so."

In the distance, the sound of dirt bikes growling up and

down a steep slope chattered across the fields. Carly's hair was probably flying in the wind as she rode, keeping up with Brett.

What would she tell me?

I think you already know.

I rolled onto my stomach and rested my chin in my hands. Danyel was the kind of guy who didn't mind when silences fell. He gazed into the hazy golden distance, giving me space while I struggled against the ropes of a promise no girl should have to keep.

Why should I have to make this decision? What a waste of time and emotion. I should be plotting on how to get Danyel to kiss me, like a normal girl.

But no. According to my dad, I wasn't a normal girl and never had been. I was a princess-in-training without even knowing about it.

Danyel chuckled, almost too low to hear.

"What?"

"I was just thinking about that verse in First Peter that talks about us being part of a royal family. You've been a princess your whole life without even knowing it."

I rolled to a sitting position, staring at him. "What did you say? Do you, like, read minds?"

"Here." He pulled his BlackBerry out of his pocket and brought up the Internet, then the Bible site I'd seen Carly using when she was supposed to be studying.

"But you are a chosen people, a royal priesthood, a holy nation, a people belonging to God, that you may declare the praises of him who called you out of darkness into his wonderful light."

"That's weird," I breathed. "I was just thinking how I wasn't normal—that my parents have been bringing me up to be this royal somebody I don't want to be."

"And all this time God had a bigger plan. He already thinks you're a princess. You've just been living like one of those ex-pats, in a foreign country. But I think you're on the way home, aren't you?"

Home.

I'd always thought it was Chicago. Lately I've thought it was San Francisco. But maybe it wasn't either of those places. Maybe it wasn't a place at all. Maybe it was a person.

Or a Being.

Or both.

I hated the thought of being a princess in the eyes of my parents, and even those of the people over there in Yasir. But being a princess in the eyes of God was completely different. It made me feel . . . wanted. Loved. Like I'd been handed a spar-kly tiara to wear on the inside, just because I was me.

I took a deep breath. "I think I know what I'm going to do."

Danyel nodded. "You'll tell me if you need me, right?"

"Believe me, you'll be the second one to know."

TEXT MESSAGE ─────────────────────────────

Beryl Hanna	If you don't answer your messages I'm calling the police.
Shani Hanna	Chill, Mom. I'm in Napa with friends.
Beryl Hanna	What?! Why aren't you in SF talking to your father and me? Irresponsible!
Shani Hanna	Needed some space.
Beryl Hanna	The dr. said rest.
Shani Hanna	I am resting. Thinking. Making a decision.
Beryl Hanna	Care to let me in on it?
Shani Hanna	Meet you at school Sunday night, 7:00 p.m. Visitors' study.
Beryl Hanna	Finally some sense.

chapter 20

ANYEL CARRIED MY BAG up Spencer's front steps and into the reception hall. Only he forgot to put it down. Instead, turning a three-sixty, he stared up at the marble staircase, at the row of French windows opening out on the grassy quad, at the carved wooden doors leading to the administration offices (which, since it was Sunday afternoon, were closed).

"You call this a school?"

"Welcome to Spencer Academy." Lissa and Gillian passed him on their way up the stairs. "No boys allowed past this point."

"Want me to take that up?" Carly grabbed my bag out of his hand and hefted it. "You should give him a tour."

Through the windows, I caught a glimpse of Rashid at one of the tables in the quad with Vanessa. A stack of books sat beside them, and as he pointed something out in her notebook, he made explanatory gestures with his hands.

Ha. Vanessa wasn't exactly short on brains. I'd bet a *crème brulée* she was playing dumb to get him to hang with her, out there where everyone on four floors could look down and see them.

Danyel watched me watching Rashid. "Who's the chick?"

I shrugged. "Random royalty. Come on, I'm starving. Let's get you a visitor pass and then raid the dining room."

We collected pass and snacks and I gave him the twenty-five-cent tour of the main building. We were down in the music wing, where Danyel had gotten a kick out of plinking out the melody to some old Beach Boys song on one of the concert harps, when we met a gaggle of seniors in the hall outside, carrying sheet music like they'd been at rehearsal.

"Is that her?" one of them asked.

"Yeah, it is." DeLayne Geary stuck out a hip and propped a hand on it. "The PG Princess herself." The others fanned out behind her, blocking the corridor so Danyel and I couldn't get past without hip-checking someone out of the way.

I mimicked her pose—which was a lot more convincing on me, let me tell you. "What are you saying? Let us by."

"I hear you been doing bad things, nasty girl."

"I hear you crazy," I retorted in her same fake street vernacular. "Give me specifics or shut up."

"Preggo." Dani Lavigne stepped out from under Rory Stapleton's arm. *Eww.* "Preg-go, preg-go." The rest took up the chant. "Preggo, preggo!"

This was not the Italian word for "you're welcome," which slipped out of Mrs. Loyola now and again. I stared at them, completely incredulous that a stupid rumor was still making the rounds—and that anyone with a brain believed it.

"Let's see that baby bump!"

"Who's your baby daddy, Hanna? The prince?"

"No way. He dumped her 'cuz she was cheating on him with this guy."

"Who is that?"

"Yeah, Shani. You two-timin' Rashid with this fine brotha? That why he dumped you?"

"I'm not your brother," Danyel told DeLayne, his lip curling with disgust. "Get out of the way, trashmouth."

"You ain't seen trash 'til you've seen this girl," DeLayne told him smugly, flicking a hand at me. "You gonna show us that bump or not?"

"I don't have to show you anything. If you believe that old rumor, you're just too stupid to live."

Danyel's face had gone from surprise to disgust to still, cold anger. "Who's saying she's pregnant?" he demanded. "Who's spreading this around?"

"Why do you care?" some boy in the back jeered. "You in lo-o-ove?"

"I care because she's my friend," Danyel snapped. "But you wouldn't know anything about that."

"Nahhh," the boy said. "Maybe you care 'cuz it's yours, huh? She doin' both of you?"

Danyel went for him, and I grabbed his arm and dragged him back.

"Doesn't matter who started it. Every rumor has some truth to it." DeLayne stared me in the eye while I kept Danyel in the edge of my vision in case he tried to jump the other kid again. "So you gonna prove us wrong?"

"You deaf? I don't have to prove anything to you. But if you had eyes in your head you'd see I'm wearing size two jeans, and there's no room for a baby." I raked her up and down with a scornful look. "Unlike some of us, who could fit a whole other person in our jeans if we'd lose some weight."

"Shani," Danyel said, one tone up from a whisper. "Don't lose it. Don't be like them."

Don't lose it? Hadn't he almost lost it? I had a lot more right to—I'd just been accused of doing the nasty with not one guy, but two!

I hunched my shoulders. "Get out of my way, scovel," I snapped, and pushed past DeLayne. The boy beside her was no match for me. I swung a hip at him and he stumbled to the right, clearing enough room for Danyel to shove past him, right behind me.

We cleared the mob and headed down the corridor, their jeers and catcalls following us like a cloud of wasps.

"Who were those people?" Danyel demanded, jogging after me.

I wasn't quite sure where I was going. I turned right, then left. "Just scumballs." The words were hard in my mouth. "Ignore them."

"It's pretty hard to ignore that."

"I've been doing it for weeks. Somebody got jealous of me and Rashid and didn't have enough imagination to do anything but start a rumor."

We were in the corridor behind the dining room. I pushed open the discreet, unmarked door to the rain tunnel, which stretched into the dim distance. A good place to hide until I got my peace back.

Which could take until morning.

"Shani, wait. Where you going so fast?"

"I'ma show you the field house. It's at the end of this tunnel."

"You don't have to run away from them."

That stopped me. "I'm not running."

He raised his eyebrows at me with a funny little smile. "Then how come I'm puffing like a train?"

"Because you're out of shape?"

But he wasn't, and I was. Running, I mean. I stopped and leaned against the cool concrete wall, tilting my head up to inspect the boring beige ceiling.

"My life stinks so bad they can smell it in Oakland."

"I'm sorry you had to go through that."

"I'm sorry you had to see it."

"I've seen worse. I go to public school, remember?"

Okay. Point taken. "Still."

He slid an arm around me and pulled me against his chest. "Don't let them get to you. You did good, facing them down like that."

"I always thought DeLayne could have been a friend. We sort of were, in freshman year, and then she hooked up with Vanessa and turned into a—" What did Lissa call them? "A pod person."

"Her loss." He leaned his forehead against mine. "Just be with me for a minute."

I don't know how much time passed. It could have been a minute. It could have been ten, or thirty. At last Danyel stirred. "I know my timing is lousy, but . . . I have to go."

I nodded. It felt so good to be held. Especially by arms as strong as these. And his shoulder felt so good under my cheek. "I know, I know. Six hours' drive."

"I'll come back next weekend. Stay with my sister."

"Please tell me I'm not invited to breakfast."

He chuckled, and I heard it deep in his chest. "Malika's not so bad. Hang around with her enough, you'll get to like her."

"I'd rather hang around with you."

"That I'll promise."

I stayed still, breathing in the scent of his clothes. "I remember another promise you made me."

He didn't play dumb. "Yeah?"

"You gonna keep it?"

"I'm waiting for the right time."

I tilted my face up to look him in the eyes. "If ever there was a right time, it's now."

For once, he didn't have an answer. Instead, he just looked into my eyes and, oh so softly, took my chin in his hand and ran his thumb along my jaw.

"You have the softest skin," he said.

And then he lowered his mouth to mine.

MY MOTHER HAD DRESSED to impress in a royal blue— get it?—Vera Wang wool suit and Donald Pliner black-patent slingbacks. Any other time I'd have been filled with admiration that hey, this was my mom looking so fine, and my dad looking every inch the CEO in his Hugo Boss double-breasted suit.

As the situation stood, I wouldn't be parading around the school showing them off anytime soon. Especially with people popping their heads out of rooms and hissing "PG Princess!" until I wanted to scream and throw sharp objects.

Danyel had only been gone two hours and already his absence felt like a big hole inside me. Next weekend seemed an eternity away—especially considering the hurdles I had to jump before I got there.

At exactly seven o'clock, I pushed the door of the visitors' study open with one hip and carried in a tray holding a plate of madeleines and three piping-hot lattes, courtesy of the barista still on duty in the dining room.

"Hey Mom, Dad. Coffee?"

Mom loves madeleines. Her head craned toward them, while the rest of her stayed aloof until she had a bead on whether or not my attitude had changed.

Well, she could take them or leave them. I helped myself to a couple, took a latte, and folded myself onto the leather couch. "These are good," I said around a bite. "You should try one."

Mom gave in and settled onto the couch with a latte and one of the little cookies. Dad was a different story.

"I want to ask you to please not disappear like that again," he said heavily. "You scared us both to death."

Disappear? Oh. Napa. "Ms. Curzon knew where we were," I said. "Did you ask her?"

"I don't need to go through the principal to find out where my daughter is. I call her phone and expect her to answer. The first time."

"Do you have any idea what I went through?" Mom asked. "I had no idea if anyone was looking after you, where you were, if you'd had a relapse, who you were with. Honestly, Shani, you need to be more responsible and considerate of other people's feelings."

"The way you considered mine?"

I wasn't angry, honest. I wanted to know. Because now that I'd made my decision, I felt completely calm. Had it only been this morning that we'd gone to church with Mrs. Loyola (barely fitting in her Range Rover)? It seemed like years ago. Anyway, for the first time, I'd focused on what people were praying about, on the words of the songs, and on what the pastor said. No looking around at other people's clothes, no scoping out cute guys, no slouching in boredom when the pastor got long-winded.

Okay, maybe a little of that last one, because the guy really did take a long time to make his point.

But still. I came out of there feeling . . . at peace. Finally. I'd made a decision, and Carly says that peace inside is the best way to tell if it's the right one.

And Danyel's kiss had gone beyond that and confirmed it.

"Shani, we have considered you, right from the beginning," my father said. "I don't understand why you wouldn't choose a life with Rashid. He's a fine young man from a family that's known in the Middle East for being ahead of the norm in human rights. You'll have unlimited money, numerous homes, and, since I know this is important to you, couture houses courting you to wear their clothes."

"I don't care about that, Dad."

"You certainly used to."

"I've changed."

"How?" my mother asked. "How have you changed? Help us understand you, and maybe we can help you understand our position."

Ha. That was about as likely as me going to Harvard. I looked at her more closely. She was way too calm, considering the situation. Had she been popping Valium?

But . . . she wanted to listen, pharmaceuticals or not, and that didn't happen often. "In the last year I've become a different person. I've learned to care about stuff. About people. I have friends I can count on, and I have a boyfriend"— Wow, had I really said that? And it was totally true!—"who cares about me and who I think is the greatest thing on two legs."

"Okay." I could see *What does this have to do with it?* stamped all over my mother's face.

"The thing is, the girl I was last year might have gone along with it, you know? Because nothing mattered to me, and I didn't matter to anyone. So anything would have been better than where I was, right?"

"You matter deeply to us," my dad said gruffly.

"Dad, you say that, but face it, if I really did, you'd put me before PetroNova or the Sheikh or Rashid or the next outfit Mom buys. Okay? You'd put me before everything else, the way Carly's dad thinks of her and her brother first before he makes decisions, or the way Mac's mom flies halfway across the world so she can be with her when she testifies, even though it hurts her worse than anything to be in that courtroom. You see what I'm saying?"

Clearly they had no idea what I was talking about, and I didn't feel like bringing them up to date on what was happening in my friends' lives.

"Anyway, the point is, the person I am now has things to live for. Plans. People. Changes to make, starting with me. You want me to be a princess in the world's eyes, but I already am in God's eyes. And speaking of that, I don't want to take World Religions. Gillian's taking me to buy some Bible study books and I'll read those instead."

Now they stared at me as if I'd sprouted another head. "What? Since when did you get religion?"

"I haven't 'got' religion. But it's kinda the only thing in my life that's making any sense, so I'ma go with it. See where it takes me."

"What does that mean?" my dad asked. He wasn't looking so good. In fact, he looked as if he needed one of Mom's pills.

"It means I'm not going to marry Rashid," I said quietly. "I'm not going to Yasir. I'm totally and completely sorry about the Sheikh pulling his stake in PetroNova, but Dad, you made that deal with him. Not me."

Silence.

More silence.

At last, through clenched teeth, my father said, "You realize what this is going to mean to your lifestyle?" He said the last word as if it tasted bad.

I swallowed. "Yes. Is the rest of term paid for?" I wasn't ready to go back to Chicago and start public school next week. If the term wasn't paid for, I was coming up with Plan B ASAP.

"Yes." He had difficulty getting the word out. "You can stay here until Christmas break. You're not getting away with this, Shani."

I gave him a long look. "You can't force me, Dad. And Rashid wouldn't take me under those circumstances, anyway."

"Have you asked him? Do you even care how he feels about this?" His voice began to rise.

"I do care. And I'm going to ask him. But I felt you should know first."

His jaw was so tight he could hardly speak, and his hands shook. I slid my feet to the floor in case he tried something on, and did a fast calculation of the distance to the door. He'd never hit me before, but I'd never destroyed his life before, either.

"Shani, I'm asking you one last time. If you refuse this, I swear I will take away everything you ever cared about. Not just this school or our house. You'll never see these friends of yours again. There will be no money. No allowance. No phone or computer to replace the ones you have. All you'll have will be the clothes on your back, because when we clear that house, I'm giving all your things to charity."

Everything I valued most—all the things I couldn't live without—were upstairs in my room.

"I understand that, Dad."

"I hope you do. Because I will never, ever forgive you for this."

I looked at him steadily. "That's okay, Dad. Because someday, somehow, at least I'll be able to forgive *you*."

SHanna	Are you busy? I need to talk.
RAmir	I have a commitment.
SHanna	Tomorrow then? After school?
RAmir	Meet me in the library. The French section.
SHanna	I have Individual Voice 6th period but it always ends early. See you at 3pm.
SHanna	Thanks.

chapter 21

I COULD SEE why Rashid had picked the French section. It was completely empty, and so far behind the stacks that Mrs. Lynn—or anyone else—wouldn't be able to hear us.

I'd only gotten through a couple of e-mail messages on my iPhone when he stepped around a bookcase and pulled out a chair next to me at the study table.

With a smile, he said, "I am sorry to be late."

"It's okay. This isn't a conversation I wanted to rush into, anyway." I slipped my phone into my bag and turned to face him.

"That does not sound good." He gave me the once-over. "Are you well? Have you recovered from your accident?"

I nodded. "With all the painkillers, I can't feel a thing. The bruises are big and ugly, but other than that, I'm good. Thanks for the flowers, by the way. I have the last of them in my room."

"It was the least I could do. When I called the hospital, they said only family were to be allowed in. And I am not . . . yet . . . your family."

Well, there was an opener if I ever heard one. "About that, Rashid."

"It is this you wish to talk about?"

I nodded. "Have you met my parents?"

He hesitated, as if he wanted to give a different answer. "Yes. They have been frequent visitors to Yasir over the last several years."

"Did you know they were here?"

"Of course. They were kind enough to invite me to dinner while you were away."

I bet they were. "Did they tell you what they told me?"

"They told me you were now aware of the agreement between our families. When I got your IM, I suspected this was to be the subject of our conversation."

"How do you feel about it? The agreement?"

I knew what my parents thought he thought. But I wanted to know how invested he was in having me as his princess before I gave him the news that I wasn't signing up for the job.

"I have not been brought up in the American way," he said slowly. "Like many sons of royal houses, I have always known I would marry for political reasons, or for family obligation. So when I came to America to meet you, I had only the memories of my childhood friend in Greece. I knew nothing of what you were like now except your appearance. I have seen your school pictures every year, you see."

In spite of myself, I made a yucky face. "About ninth grade. I'm so sorry. That was a bad hair day."

He chuckled. "The picture from last year more than made up for it. I looked forward to meeting you again for months."

"I don't regret it," I told him softly. "Our meeting, I mean. I hope you know that. You're one of the nicest guys I've ever known."

"I, too, enjoyed getting to know you." Those deep brown eyes gazed into mine. "But I fear we are sounding like good-bye."

"I fear we are." I took a deep breath. "I can't go through with our fathers' agreement. I can't marry you, Rashid."

He straightened, and I could swear it was because a huge load had just been lifted from his shoulders. But he didn't break his gaze. "Why not, Shani?"

"Because we're too young, for starters. And even if we waited until after we got out of college, I still couldn't do it. I want more than political reasons and family obligation. I want love and happiness and everything that comes with spending your life with the one person you can't live without."

"Am I not . . . lovable?"

Of all the questions he could have asked me, this was one I hadn't expected. A lump formed in my throat and I felt the hot tears welling in my eyes. "Of course you are, Rashid. You're gorgeous and rich and sweet and a complete gentleman, and you kiss like nobody's business. Someday, some girl is going to be lucky enough to fall for you, and she'll be everything you deserve." I wiped the stupid tear away. "I'm really sorry I'm not that girl. I wish I could have been, because it would make everyone happy. But I'm not."

"You are sure of this?"

I nodded and touched his hand. "I'm sure."

With a sigh, he looked down at my hand with its stubby nails Lissa had tried to repair for me last night. "My father will blame me," he said. "He will say I did not try hard enough."

"You tell your dad to call me. I'll set him straight. You're everything a girl could want in a handsome prince. It's not your fault I fell for a surfer boy long before I ever met you."

"Ah. The one I met at Due that night?"

"Uh-huh."

"At least my father will understand that. He will not like it, but he will understand it. And I have something to confess, as well."

"What's that?"

"I, too, believe there may be someone else. It is too soon

to know, but if you mean what you say, then I am free to find out."

Vanessa? DeLayne? Some other girl? Whoever she was, I hoped she lived up to him. "Um. Back to your dad. Do you think he'll go through with pulling his stake out of my dad's company?"

"Oh, yes. The Sheikh has a deal, and he will make sure every last point of the contract is followed." From the sound of it, Rashid had had a little experience along that line. I guess I wasn't the only one with a father who put business ahead of family.

"I guess I'd better prepare myself for changes, then." I slouched in the studded leather library chair. "Like going to public school and being disowned."

His eyebrows rose. "Disowned?"

With a nod, I rehashed what my father had told me.

"But this is terrible," he said. "How can he punish you in this way?"

"I don't think he's punishing me, not really. The consequences are what they are, and he wants me to know that. I mean, most people just give back the ring when they decide not to get married. With you and me, the consequences are . . . bigger. It's not either of our faults that our dads made a deal with strings attached. We still have to live with it."

He gazed at me, and I thought I saw a glimmer of admiration in his eyes. "I could not live with it."

"I don't know if I can, either. But I'm going to try. I'll show him. I'll get into Harvard without his money or his help. There's a reason for all those scholarships."

He smiled. "You would have made a fine princess, you know."

I had to smile, too. "Maybe. Just not the right one for you." This seemed to be as good a moment as any. "Rashid, I need to give you back your necklace." I reached into my bag and pulled out the velvet box Ms. Curzon had been keeping for me.

Then I hesitated and cracked it open to take one last look. The diamonds glittered happily at me under the library lights. "Take it before I run out of here with it." I closed the box and handed it to him.

"You are welcome to keep it."

"Are you kidding? I know about the Star of the Desert. No way am I hanging onto a family heirloom. It goes to your bride, whoever she turns out to be."

He slipped the box into an inner pocket in his jacket. "The woman who most deserves to wear the Star will not accept it. I am very sorry for that."

"Don't be sorry, Rashid. Be glad we were friends. Be glad we still can be. On the day you get married, you can expect a nice box from Bloomingdale's or Tiffany, even if I have to save up for ten years to give it to you."

With a laugh, he leaned over and kissed me on the cheek. For one last time, I paused to appreciate the feel of his lips and the scent of his mad expensive cologne.

"I will make a special point of looking for it, Shani." He pulled me to my feet. "Good-bye."

I hugged him, just because I could and no one was looking. "Good-bye, Rashid. See you in American Diplomacy."

And I watched the handsome prince turn and walk away from me.

Cue the violins.

From the *Wall Street Journal*, October 29, 2009

PetroNova Stock Slashed In Half

In an unprecedented tumble, stock in petroleum exploration firm PetroNova (LSE:PTNV) fell by almost fifty percent on the news that the Sheikh of Yasir, its primary source of capital, was pulling his backing out of the company.

While CEO Roger Hanna was not available for comment due to a family emergency, CFO Sarah Leonard told the press, "The Sheikh's contributions to Petro-Nova in terms of capital, exploration freedom in Yasir, and his wise decisions on our Board of Directors have been instrumental in the success of this company. However, he is anxious to explore other ventures in the area of environmental reform, and we understand his decision not to proceed with a third round of venture capital."

Leonard went on, "I want to reassure our stockholders that PetroNova is a completely viable investment."

The market would appear to disagree. With its value down by half, the Board will be forced to reorganize, and it is likely Hanna will be ousted from his position at the helm.

From the *Chicago Tribune*, November 18, 2009

Layoff Cripples Local Firm

PetroNova, one of the most successful independent oil exploration firms in the world, stands poised on the brink of disaster—or a new era. But from the point of view of the 2,000 employees who were affected by a reduction in force this week, it's definitely the former.

The anchor firm in the Bering Business Park, the five-year-old company had just reached the billion-dollar value milestone last year. But with the departure of its primary stakeholder, the Sheikh of Yasir, last month, the Cinderella story came to an end.

CEO Roger Hanna, a regular in the on-court seats at Bulls games and a frequent and generous contributor to charities citywide, is a changed man. He appeared haggard during our interview, but remained upbeat. "It was time for a change," he said. The spacious corner office was filled with packing boxes, and it was obvious that Hanna had been among the 2,000 employees receiving pink slips. "I'll be forming a new company based on our small but active abandonment division. Going back to my roots and doing what I've always wanted to do—cleaning up well sites after companies like PetroNova are finished with exploration and drilling. I feel I can make important contributions to saving our environment in this new field."

When asked about his feelings about the Sheikh's decision, Hanna was tight-lipped. "I can't speak for His Highness, who is entitled to do what he wants with his money. I'm just doing the best I can for my family and what's left of my company."

With the recent sales of his multimillion-dollar home, the corporate jet, and his antique automobile collection, the former CEO made sure his employees got their final paychecks. Philanthropic gestures aside, it's not certain he will be able to secure funding for his startup. In this economic climate, banks may not look with a favorable eye on the engineer of a collapse such as the one suffered by PetroNova. It's also not clear if the skeleton crew of about forty people left on the site will stay to help him in the new venture.

Chicago will miss the man who was Entrepreneur of the Year in 2005. "One thing is for sure," said one departing employee who asked not to be named. "PetroNova will miss him. I'm glad I won't be working here if Roger's gone."

POP! POP-POP-POPPITY-POP.

Lissa's dad, Gabe Mansfield, tried not to squint against the barrage of flash from a zillion cameras. While he waited for us next to the limo door, we scrambled out one after the other— Lissa and Kaz, Gillian and Jeremy, Carly and Brett, and me, Mac, and Danyel.

"Holy freaking ravioli," Danyel muttered as he helped Mac out and offered each of us an arm. "This is like Armageddon."

"Hardly," Mac retorted through a brilliant smile. "Shani, can I tell you again how fabulous you look?"

"As many times as you want," I said. "I think we all look so fine we'll get our own spread again in *People*."

Because last week I'd picked up a voice mail from my mom. "Don't tell your father about this," she said, her words rushed and quiet. "But before we left Paris the last time, I bought your birthday present. Your father is giving your things to charity, but he doesn't know about this. I know you haven't forgiven me, and I know you're monitoring your calls, but I'm doing this anyway. I'm FedExing it to you so you can wear it to the premiere."

The box had come the next day, and inside it was no less than an *haute couture* gown, designed for me by Karl Lagerfeld himself and made to my exact measurements.

Lissa and Mac had both swooned with admiration. I wasn't so sure I even wanted to wear it. It seemed too much like putting a Band-Aid on a sliced artery, you know? But then I thought, she could have sold it at auction to make a down payment on a house, and she didn't. So in the end I decided to wear it, like a last hurrah for the way things used to be.

"Check it out, guys," Carly said, jerking her chin to the left. "*ET*'s interviewing Lissa's parents."

"Parents plural?" I blurted. "Where'd her mom come from?"

But no one knew. She certainly hadn't been in the limo with us, but you know what? From the expression on Gabe's face, he didn't care if she'd been beamed down onto the red carpet by aliens.

"That's an Armani Couture dress," Carly whispered. "Doesn't she look fabu in ice blue?" Then she looked at Lissa. "Lissa? *Amiga*, are you okay?"

Lissa fumbled in her jeweled evening bag, her breathing jerky. "Oh, no. I didn't bring any—"

Carly handed her a tissue. "We're all going to need these anyway, from what I've seen on the trailers. What's wrong?"

"Nothing. I mean that." She smiled as she tried to dab tears away, keeping her back to the *Entertainment Tonight* camera crew. "I didn't think she would come. Dad was convinced she wouldn't. But she did."

I stole a peek at Patricia Sutter, who clung firmly to Gabe's arm and smiled up at him as Lara Spencer fired question after question. "What happened, do you think?"

Lissa shook her head. "I don't know." She glanced at Kaz. "We're sitting with them, whatever happens."

"Done."

"We're all sitting together," Gillian said. "Lissa got Gabe's executive assistant to send us the seating chart. And guess who's in the row in front of us?"

"Who?" Jeremy asked.

"Ewan MacGregor and Orlando Bloom!"

We girls went, "Squeeee!" while the boys rolled their eyes.

And then suddenly *The Insider* got into our faces. "And this looks like Gabe Mansfield's entourage," Steven Cojocaru said with a huge smile. "Who do we have here? And I must know what you're wearing."

Lissa stuffed the tissue into her bag and morphed into the Hollywood royalty she is. "I'm his daughter, Lissa, and this is graphic artist Kaz Griffin. Next to him is fashion designer Carly Aragon."

"Yeah? Who are you wearing, Carly?"

"I'm wearing my own design," Carly said quietly. "I made it when I interned with Tori Wu in San Francisco this past summer."

The camera crew swirled around her, and I knew Carly's phone would be ringing off the hook by Monday as the fashion magazines descended like a flock of magpies. I knew she planned to apply to FIDM and Parsons, so this would fatten up her clip portfolio big time.

"And what about you?" Steven said to me. "Are you enjoying the view here on the red carpet? Who are you wearing? What's your name?"

"I'm Shani Hanna, and I'm wearing Karl Lagerfeld *couture*, from Paris," I said as if it totally didn't matter. "And I'm having a wonderful time here with all my best friends."

"Hanna?" His eyes sharpened on me. "Are you the Shani Hanna whose name was linked to the Prince of Yasir?" I nodded. He obviously knew the truth, so no point trying to keep it on the down low. "Miss Hanna, do you mind if I ask you a few questions?"

I glanced at Gabe and Patricia, who were already moving on up the ropes to the next interview. "Um, if we're quick. I don't want to lose the rest of my party."

Reaching behind me, I grabbed Danyel's hand for support.

"I'll just keep you a minute. Miss Hanna, is it true you were engaged to the prince?"

I smiled a professional smile. "Not at all."

"You must be up on the gossip. It's been reported that he's now seeing the daughter of the Principessa di Firenze, who goes to Spencer Academy. Can you confirm that?"

"I can, Steve. They seem very happy together." Which was the truth. Rashid's mystery girl wasn't such a mystery after all. Vanessa—believe it or not—had found someone who demanded that she be real. Rashid didn't put up with any of her snot-nosed garbage, and she'd started showing signs of becoming an actual human being. It would probably end if and when they broke up, but in the meantime, Spencer was heaving a sigh of relief.

"Miss Hanna, that Harry Winston necklace looks too, too familiar. Wasn't that the diamond cluster piece given to you by His Highness?"

"The original was," I said.

He snapped his fingers and looked into the camera a moment. "That's what's different. Girlfriend, what happened to the Star of the Desert? It seems to be missing."

But at that moment, Gabe turned and waved at us urgently, flashing "five minutes" with his fingers. Five minutes to curtain and the beginning of *The Middle Window*, and we weren't seated yet. His handlers swarmed around us and herded us away from the TV crews.

I tossed a smile at Steven over my shoulder and Danyel and I hurried toward the yawning cavern that was the entrance to the Kodak Theatre.

It was none of the world's business what I wore around my throat. This was its last appearance, anyway. From now on, any diamonds in my future would be the kind I paid for with my own hard-earned money, sometime out there in the future, once I had my M.B.A. and my career was on its way. Or maybe I'd get one from a certain special person who might wear Danyel's smile, or might not.

I was leaving all that up to God. Because He'd worked a miracle.

I settled into the plush seat in the middle of the theater, all my friends talking and rustling and arranging their pretty dresses around me as we settled down. Inside I felt a warm, glowing calm. Thanksgiving was next week, and I had more invites than I knew what to do with—from Mrs. Loyola, from Carly's dad, from Lissa. But there was only one place I really wanted to be: at Danyel's parents' place in Santa Barbara. Malika wouldn't be cooking the turkey, which meant there was a chance it'd be the real thing.

This time last year I'd jetted off to Bermuda for the long weekend. By myself. But the days of jetting anywhere, alone or not, were over.

And you know what? I was good with that. I had my friends, I had Danyel, and I had the rest of my senior year, guaranteed, at Spencer Academy. I even had this couture dress for special occasions. I might wear it out and everyone would get tired of looking at it, but that was okay, too.

So, you probably want to know about that miracle, right? I don't know if it was Rashid's idea or the Big Guy's, but the day before yesterday I received a velvet box by special courier. Inside was the Winston diamond cluster necklace—minus the Star of the Desert.

On top of it lay a letter.

Delivered by hand
November 19, 2009

Shani, my dear friend,

As you advised me, the Star of the Desert
has gone back to Yasir to wait for my bride,
whoever she might be. But when I ordered
this necklace, it was for you. I would very
much like you to have it as a token of my
high esteem for your friendship, your honesty, and your integrity. You have opened
up my life to make it as I choose, and for
that I will always be grateful.

   I have left instructions with Harry Winston that if by chance the necklace were
to come back, they are to refund you the
full purchase price. I understand that college educations are expensive, especially
at Harvard Business School. But I believe
that two million dollars will take you a
long way toward your goal—and beyond that,
you will have a nice sum to begin your life
with after college.

   We have set each other free, my friend.

Go with God.
Rashid

about the author

Shelley Adina wrote her first teen novel when she was thirteen. It was rejected by the literary publisher to whom she sent it, but he did say she knew how to tell a story. That was enough to keep her going through the rest of her adolescence, a career, a move to another country, a B.A. in Literature, an M.A. in Writing Popular Fiction, and countless manuscript pages.

Shelley is a world traveler and pop culture junkie with an incurable addiction to designer handbags. She knows the value of a relationship with a gracious God and loving Christian friends and loves writing about fun and faith—with a side of glamour. Between books, Shelley loves traveling, listening to and making music, and watching all kinds of movies.

IF YOU LIKED

who made you a princess?

you'll love the fifth book in the All About Us series:

tidings of great boys

available in September 2009!

Turn the page for a sneak peek…

chapter 1

SOME PEOPLE are born with the gift of friendship. Some achieve it. And then you have people like me, who have friendship thrust upon them.

Believe me, there's no one happier about that than I am—in fact, I probably wouldn't be alive right now without it—but it wasn't always that way. My name is Lindsay Margaret Eithne MacPhail, and because my dad is a Scottish earl, that makes my mother a countess and me a lady.

I know. Stop laughing.

To my friends I'm simply Mac. If you call me Lady Lindsay I'll think you're (1) being pretentious, or (2) announcing me at a court ball, and since none of my friends are likely to do either, let's keep it Mac between us, all right?

This all started when I sat in the the dark, deserted computer lab and watched the timestamp on the monitor click over: eleven o'clock.

"Carrie?" I settled the earphones on my head and leaned toward the microphone pickup.

"All right?" Her familiar voice came over Skype and I smiled, even though she couldn't see it. She sounded like sleepovers and mischief and long walks through the woods and heath. Like rain and mist and Marmite on toast. She sounded like home.

"Yeah." I swallowed the lump in my throat. I'd chosen to come to Spencer Academy for the fall term instead of going back to St. Cecelia's. I'd hounded my mother and when that didn't work, my dad. So I had no business being homesick. Besides, being all weepy just wasted precious minutes. Carrie had to leave for school and I had to sneak back up to the third floor without the future Mrs. Milsom, our dorm mistress, catching me after lights-out.

"Only two weeks to go until you're home," Carrie said. "I'm already planning all the things we're going to do. Anna Grange has a new flat in Edinburgh and she says we can come crash anytime we like. Gordon and Terrell can't wait to see you—they want to take us to a new club. And—"

"Hang on." How to put this? "I haven't actually decided what I'm doing for winter break. There's a lot going on here."

Silence crackled in my headset. "What nonsense. You always come home. Hols are the only time I ever get to see you—not to mention all your other mates. What do you mean, a lot going on?"

"Things to do, people to see," I said, trying to soften the blow. "Mummy wants me in London, of course, since she hasn't had me for nearly three months. And I have invitations to Los Angeles and New York."

"From who?"

"A couple of the girls here."

The quality of the silence changed. "And these girls—they wouldn't be the ones splashed all over *Hello!* last month, would they? At some Hollywood premiere or other?"

"Oddly, yes. I told you all about it when that issue came out."

She made a noise in her throat that could have been disgust or sheer disparagement of my taste. "That's fine, then. If you'd rather spend your vay-cay-shun with your Hollywood friends, it's nowt to me."

"Carrie, I haven't said I'd go. I just haven't made up my mind."

As changeable as a sea wind, her temper veered. "You must come. We're all dying to see you. I saw your dad in the village and he invited all of us particularly as soon as you get home."

"Did he?"

"I know. I didn't think he'd even remember who I was, but he stopped me in the door of the chip shop and told me I was to come. He sounded so excited."

This did not sound like my dad, who wasn't exactly a recluse, but wasn't in the habit of accosting random teenagers in chip shops and inviting them up to the house either. She was probably having me on. I had a lot of practice in peering behind Carrie's words for what she really wanted. She was my friend, and friends wanted to be with each other.

The problem was, I had more friends now than I used to. Besides the ones at Strathcairn and in London, there were the ones here at Spencer. And lately, Carly, Shani, Lissa, and Gillian were turning out to be solid—more so than any friends I'd had before.

Awkward.

"I'll let you know as soon as I figure out what I'm doing," I told Carrie. "I've got to go. The Iron Maiden stalks the halls."

Carrie laughed. "Love the pic you sent with your camera phone. What a horror. Who would marry her?"

"The Bio prof, apparently. The wedding's set for New Year's Eve to take advantage of some tax benefit or other."

"How bleedin' romantic."

There was another Christmas wedding in the works, but I hadn't heard much about it lately. Carly Aragon's mum was supposed to marry some braw lad she'd met on a cruise ship, much to Carly's disgust. I could relate, a little. If my mother was going to marry a man who looked like a relic from an eighties pop band, I'd be a little upset, too. So far Carly was refusing to be bridesmaid, and the big day was sneaking up on her fast.

"I'll call you at the weekend."

"I might be busy."

"Then I'll call Gordon and Terrell. I know *they* love me."

She blew me a raspberry and signed off. Still smiling, I laid the headphones on the desk and got up.

And froze as a thin, dark shape moved in the doorway. The lights flipped on.

I blinked and squinted as Ms. Tobin stared me down. "I thought I heard voices. Is there someone here with you?" I shook my head. "You do realize, Lady Lindsay, that lights-out is ten o'clock? And it is now twenty after eleven?"

"I'll take your word for it."

"What are you doing in here?"

"Calling home."

She scanned the rows of silent computers. Not a telephone to be seen. "And you can't do that from the privacy of your own room?"

"It's eleven twenty and my roommates are asleep," I pointed out helpfully. "But it's seven twenty in Scotland. I use Skype so there are no long distance charges."

She rolled her eyes up, as if doing the math. "Calling Scotland? Your family?"

I smiled. If I didn't actually answer, I wouldn't be lying. "My

B.T. phone doesn't work over here, so I use Skype." I let the smile falter. "I get homesick."

Ms. Tobin pinned me with her gaze like a butterfly on a board. "I sympathize, but you still broke a school rule. A demerit will be added to your record. Again."

Oh, please. Who cared about demerits when I needed to talk to Carrie? "I'm sorry, Ms. Tobin."

"Come along. I'll escort you to your room."

And she did, like a bad-tempered Dementor floating along beside me. Only compared to that dreadful brown tweed skirt and round-toed Oxfords, the Dementors were turned out in haute couture. Did the woman actually have on knee-high stockings?

"Good night, Lady Lindsay."

I shuddered and shut the door, locking it for good measure.

"Mac?" Carly's sleepy voice came from the direction of her bed, muffled by a quilt. "Who's that with you?"

"I called home and got caught," I whispered. "Ms. Tobin marched me up here."

Carly groaned.

I undressed and crawled into bed. Shani, Carly, and I made do in a room designed for two. I have to admit it was kind of fun rooming with those two. Since her debacle with the heir to the Lion Throne last month, Shani has lost a little of her attitude. She doesn't look at people with scornful eyes like she used to, and when she talks, it's to you and not at you.

Or maybe it's just me.

I returned to the problem at hand. With two weeks left to go before the holidays, what was I to do? Home or here? Old or new? Family or friends? And really, what was the difference?

I blinked and stiffened on my goosedown pillow.

That was it. There was no difference. My family and my friends all belonged together. With me. At home.

"Carly?" I whispered. "Are you awake?"

"Guhhhm."

"Do you think everyone would like to come to Scotland with me for Christmas?"

"DEFINE *EVERYONE*." Gillian leaned across her dish of oatmeal and took a peach out of the bowl on the table.

I swallowed a spoonful of yogurt before I answered. I hadn't put a single molecule of porridge near my mouth since I arrived in the States. I'd had sixteen years of it, thank you very much, and there was no one here to make me eat the stuff.

Lissa dived into my hesitation. "You don't really mean that, do you? All of us? At Strathcairn?"

"I do mean it. We have fourteen bedrooms, not counting the old nurseries and the staff floor. Those are closed off, anyway. The beds might be a little dusty, but if I let my dad know right away, he can get some of the ladies from the village to come tidy things up. There are plenty of rooms and tons of things to do."

"Like what?" Carly put away oatmeal at a scary rate. I shuddered.

"Like skating on the pond and cross-country skiing. And parties." I saw the Strathcairn of ten years ago, when Mum had been the most spectacular hostess the old pile had seen in generations. "Lots of parties and balls and live bands and whatever we want."

"Don't tell me," Shani said. "You're going to teach us Sir Roger de Coverley, aren't you?"

"No, that's for babies," I said scornfully. What did she know about country dances? "I'll teach you Strip the Willow before we go so you don't make utter fools of yourselves."

"Whatever. Doesn't sound like my thing." She fished the last blueberry out of her fruit cup. Something in her face told me what the real problem was.

"If you're worried about the money, don't. We'll work it out."

"How are you gonna do that?" Her dark eyes looked guarded. She may have been dumped by her parents for refusing to go through with an arranged marriage, but her pride wasn't dented one bit.

"You don't have to touch your nest egg. My allowance ought to cover a plane ticket. First class, of course."

"Hmph." Shani crossed her arms over her chest and looked away.

I knew she had a cool two million socked away in the San Francisco branch of the Formosa-Pacific Bank, and that one of Gillian's dozens of cousins was her personal investment advisor. But she treated that money like it was two hundred instead of two million, watching over it with sharp eyes that didn't let a single cent escape without accounting for itself.

Lissa glanced at Carly, who was eating and not talking, like she hoped we wouldn't notice her. She's a master of the art of the personal fade. "And mine can cover Carly's," she said.

"Let's throw mine in and split two fares three ways," Gillian said. "Easy peasy."

"For you, maybe," Carly mumbled. "Brett's already asked me to spend Christmas with his family. Consequently my dad didn't just blow a fuse, he totally blew out the power grid."

"What is with your dad?" I demanded. "I've never seen anyone so protective. I'd die if I was smothered like that."

"She isn't smothered," Shani said with a glance across the table at Carly. "Between my dad and hers, I'd take hers any day. At least he cares."

"Is it guilt talking?" Lissa wanted to know. "The whole, 'I'm out of town ninety percent of the time, so we have to spend every minute of the ten percent together'?"

"I guess." Carly sipped her honey latte. "So if he had that kind of fit about me spending Christmas sixty miles away, guess what he'd say about going to another continent?"

"Good point." I refused to take no for an answer, though. "But what about you personally?" Never mind. I answered the obvious myself. "I guess if you had the choice, you'd pick Brett."

"Not necessarily." She smiled at me, that warm Carly smile that makes puppies and old people and prickly Scots love her. "His house is nice, but it's no castle."

Lissa laughed. "I bet it has central heating, though."

"Strathcairn has central heating." I tried not to sound defensive. "In the new part, and the kitchen. But there's a fireplace in every room."

"I'm not putting wood on a fire and getting smoke in all my clothes." Lissa held up a "stop it right there" hand.

"Not a wood fire, you numpty, a gas fire." I looked at them all. "Honestly, what else has she been telling you?"

"Just that it was cold," Gillian offered. "Forty degrees, I think she said. And that was inside."

I pretended to glare at Lissa, maligning my house. "If you all came, the place would be at its best, I promise. You'll love it. And if your parents give you static, tell them to come, too."

"Ewww." Gillian looked appalled, and Shani, who has stayed in New York with Gillian's family, buried her snort of laughter in her tall glass of pomegranate juice.

"Wait a second." Lissa looked as if she'd just figured out a new way to ace a bio exam. She flipped out her phone and pressed a button. "Hey, Dad, it's me. Fine. No, nothing's wrong and no, I don't need a favor." She rolled her eyes at us. "When is the U.K. premiere of *The Middle Window*? Yes. Wow, you're kidding. That's perfect. So you're going over." She mimed smacking her forehead. "Never mind, dumb question. What about

Mom? Oh." She was silent for several seconds, blinking her contacts into place as her eyes filled. She gulped, then cleared her throat. "Well, I doubt it, but I'll try. Okay. Thanks. Yeah, I'm at breakfast. Finals this week. Need lots of protein and antioxidants and stuff to make the brain retain, you know? Love you two times. 'Bye."

All around us, the dining room rattled and silverware clashed on plates and people talked incessantly. But at our table, half a dozen pairs of eyes watched silently as Lissa tapped her phone off and put it in her glossy Kate Spade tote.

"Are you okay?" Gillian was the only one with the nerve to ask. But then, she and Lissa room together, so they probably share a lot we don't know about.

Lissa smoothed one hand over her blond hair, as if making sure her Stacey Lapidus hairband with its little rhinestone love knot was still in place. "Recovering," she said. "Stand by for reboot."

Anyone else would have said, "Give me a minute," but Lissa isn't like anyone else. None of these girls are. It's a bit weird that they've all found each other here, frankly. Or maybe not weird. Maybe inevitable. I finished my yogurt and started on my fruit cup. There's the Christian thing, of course. I used to think it wasn't my cup of tea at all, having quite a horror of Bible-thumpers and mad-eyed conviction. But these girls aren't like that at all.

They're solid, and what they believe is part of it. When I first met them, I used to try to catch them out at it. Get them to make a mistake, blow up, whatever. But I never could—at least, that they'd let me see. No matter how badly I treated them—and I can get pretty bad, as anyone will tell you—they didn't dish it back. Oh, they said a few things. No one is that good, especially considering the provocation. But we slowly became friends, and I slowly got drawn into their circle.

Which isn't a bad place to be, since they're what's considered the A-list around here. Oh, you have your Vanessas and your Danis and your DeLaynes, but they're more bark than bite. They orbit in a different universe—as a matter of fact, they've sort of gone off orbit since Vanessa started going 'round with the Prince of Yasir. What do you call it when planets lose their center of gravity and start drifting off into space? That clique is like that now.

Lissa took a deep breath and I focused on her. Recovery, evidently, was complete.

"Thing one. Dad says that the U.K. premiere is December 19. Term ends on the sixteenth. Thing two: he's going over for it, and the production team at Leavesden Studios as well as the people from Scotland are all invited. Thing three: your mom and dad are invited, too, Mac." I blinked in surprise. Dad hadn't said a thing about it, and I'd gotten an e-mail from him that morning. "And thing four: my mother says she's not going. Dad wants me to talk her into it. What do you think my chances are?"

She looked around at us, and the hope in her eyes was almost painful. I knew all about it. Been there, done that, threw away the T-shirt.

"I guess that means at least you're coming, then," I said briskly. "Because of course you'll talk your mother 'round. And once you do, your parents must come to Strathcairn afterward for Christmas. I insist."

Because if Lissa could talk her mother into coming, then I could talk mine into it as well. For the first time since the divorce.

This was going to be the best, most unforgettable Christmas ever. I'd make sure of it.